# GONE INDIAN

# Robert Kroetsch

---

# GONE INDIAN

This edition published in 1999 by Stoddart Publishing Co. Limited
34 Lesmill Road, Toronto, Canada M3B 2T6

*Distributed by:*
General Distribution Services Ltd.
325 Humber College Blvd., Toronto, Canada M9W 7C3
Tel. (416) 213-1919    Fax (416) 213-1917
Email customer.service@ccmailgw.genpub.com

new press edition published in 1973
Theytus Books edition published in 1981

03  02  01  00  99    1  2  3  4  5

**Canadian Cataloguing in Publication Data**

Kroetsch, Robert, 1927–
Gone Indian

ISBN 0-7737-6086-5

I. Title.

PS8521.R7G66 1999    C813'.54    C99-931515-3
PR9199.3.K76G66 1999

*Cover design:* Angel Guerra
*Text design:* Joseph Gisini/Andrew Smith Graphics Inc.

Printed and bound in Canada

*We acknowledge for their financial support of our publishing program the Canada Council, the Ontario Arts Council, and the Government of Canada through the Book Publishing Industry Development Program (BPIDP).*

*for*
*Ron & Pat Smith*

"For a moment, at the frontier, the bonds of
custom are broken and unrestraint is triumphant."
— Frederick Jackson Turner
"The Significance of the Frontier in American History"

48 Lathrop Avenue
Binghamton, New York 13905
*Saturday, August 19*

Miss *Jill Sunderman*
*Klondike Towers*
*Edmonton, Alberta*

*Dear Miss Sunderman,*

At the end of your letter you ask me, in your offhand manner, to "explain everything." Let me reply that I feel under no obligation to explain anything.

But I will acknowledge that Jeremy Sadness at least attempted, for a number of years, to study under my direction. As a consequence I knew his inability to get things down on paper; it was I who recommended that he take with him a tape recorder on his trip west. That way, in spare moments, he might commit to tape the meditations and insights that would help him complete his dissertation.

Instead of doing as I instructed, he used the recorder to insult everything the university must stand for. He mailed back to me a number of recordings of nothing but his own voice, along with the impertinent injunction: a) Don't listen to these tapes, b) Having listened, don't try to correct them, c) Save everything until I get back to the States.

I am transcribing a few passages from those same tapes, simply that you might better appreciate the kind of rascal you found yourself involved with. It is my own opinion that everything he says can be taken at face value. He was as surprised as are we by the course of events, failing to understand, as he did, the nature of freedom. His

1

wife, however — and I suspect he did not tell you he was married — Carol insists that he was faking everything from the moment he spoke the first sentence into the recorder. The hard academic truth was never adequate to Jeremy Sadness. Therefore she would have us distrust his original promise to "hurry back," and even the evidence of his "tragic" end.

Carol, try as she might, cannot dismiss Jeremy's romantic interest in the northern forests and the buffalo plains. Perhaps it is for that reason I sometimes on a hot evening, after grading papers or working on my nearly completed book, drive her up to the Ross Park Zoo on the hillside south of Binghamton. We walk through the smell of the caged and fenced animals, past the zebras and the dromedary, to the highest paddock. There we sit on the grass and watch the old buffalo bull, the buffalo cow. Together they stand, side by side, eating hay, drowsing, switching their tails to keep off the flies. The bull, under his horny forehead, has an almost delicate mouth. The cow has ankles of an absolutely exquisite turn, over her neat hoofs.

Last night, especially, Carol and I had dallied longer than usual. A cool breeze came through the unlikely oak trees. The far, high moon was red in the smog. Throbbing on the air came a dull and distant roar of automobiles that might have been silence itself. Or the rolling of thunder. Almost no one troubles to make the steep climb to the highest fence. We had looked at those great beasts for a long time, had speculated, even, on their trip east, had watched their tongues sweep the yellow clay of the paddock for the buffalo grass that is not to be found.

Then we ourselves, down on the blue-shadowed grass outside the fence, began to frolic, even as children might. We tussled and romped on all fours. The buffalo, I must add, came to the fence to watch us.

"It is dark enough," Carol said, "so that no one can see."

"Don't be silly," I said.

"Professor Madham," she said, "is being Professor Madham."

2

"Never," I said. "But how on earth —"

She had already slipped out of her shorts, untied her halter. She wriggled free of her panties and I caught them up as if with great bruising horns, and I tossed them aside. And yet she said to me, "Do you dare?"

"Just you close your eyes," I whispered, taking off — But already I stray from my purpose. Attached find the necessary documents. They will show me to be, so to speak, unfallen. I am my own man.

Sincerely,

*Mark*

(Professor) R. Mark Madham

# 1

Before we plunge into the inconsistencies and contradictions of the first tape, I should like to put to rest certain questions that might arise concerning my own ties both to Jeremy and to his wife. Surely the relationship between a professor and his student is a sacred one: let me be first to applaud that article of faith. But just as surely it is the task of the professor to help his student out of the nest — so to speak — and into the living world.

Jeremy believed that his whole life was shaped and governed by some deep American need to seek out the frontier. A child of Manhattan, born and bred, he dreamed always a far interior that he might in the flesh inhabit. He dreamed northwest, that is undeniable. Only let me assert: it was I who sent him there.

It was I who arranged for him the job interview at that last university in that last city on the far, last edge of our civilization. I made the discreet phone call; he merely boarded a plane. His first cassette was mailed, according to its postmark, in the Edmonton International Airport: with U.S. postage. Somehow it arrived here safely — two days after it was mailed. It begins, not with words of delight, or even gratitude —

Our dear Jeremy lost his suitcase. More precisely, he opened a suitcase for the waiting Customs official, and found the suitcase he had claimed was not his own. He responded by jerking loose the microphone of his portable tape recorder, as if he might be drawing some magical six-gun that must solve the problem.

"Hey," he said. "This isn't mine."

How appropriate that those should be his first words.

"Don't be embarrassed," the Customs man said.

"No," Jeremy said. "I mean it. This suitcase isn't mine. Mine is just like this one. Exactly like it. But in it is a very important —"

5

"Hurry along please," another Customs official said.

"Wait," Jeremy insisted. "Mine is locked." As if to prove it he jingled a veritable jailor's ring of keys.

"Have you anything to declare?"

"Nothing."

"Cigarettes? Liquor?"

"No sir."

"Where were you born?"

"New York, New York."

"How long will you be staying?"

"Two days. Maybe three."

"Purpose of trip?"

"I want to be Grey Owl."

"I beg your pardon, sir?"

"Grey Owl. I want to become —"

Jeremy Sadness might have chosen no end of frontiersmen to embody his dream of westward flight. Curiously, he chose a model from the utmost cultivated shores of the civilized world. Given as he was to self-deceiving self-analysis, he believed that his life's predicament found its type in Grey Owl. He was almost anally fascinated by that quick-tempered English lad who left Victorian England, disappeared into the Canadian bush, and emerged years later as Wa-Sha-Quon-Asin.

He-Who-Travels-By-Night.

The possibility of transformation, I must recognize, played no little part in Jeremy's abiding fantasy of fulfilment. It gave him, in the face of all his inadequacies, the illusion of hope. Yet the hopelessness of the poor boy's dreams, his sheer inability to cope, was evidenced when the Customs official flipped open a book that lay on top of a pair of red pyjamas, pointed to a page:

"Then you are not —"

6

Just for a moment, Professor, I couldn't remember my name. For a fatal moment my stumbling, ossified, PhD-seeking mind was a clean sheet. Sixty-nine uneasy middle-class smugglers were eager to have me arrested and flung into prison so they might get to hell through Customs with their loot. *"The Consolidated Rules of Court,"* I indicated sarcastically, touching a finger to a bookplate, "belongs to a Roger Dorck —"

A tap on my shoulder.

I look around.

This goddamned eight-foot Mountie is standing there.

"Come with me, son."

Son, he says. *Son.* "It isn't mine," I practically shout. "I admit it isn't mine. I'm not stealing it." My voice echoes back on my blushing ears. "Take it from me, please."

Come with me," this big RCMP repeats. Patiently. Firmly.

"I ADMIT IT ISN'T MINE."

"Sure," he says. He nods his Boy Scout hat. "It isn't yours. It never is."

Professor, I am totally innocent, a poor city boy set down by blundering jet among the wicked and the rebellious of the vanishing frontier. But the next thing I know I'm in a cubicle with the world's most beautiful blonde and we're ordered to take our clothes off.

"There's been some mistake," I assure her.

She only smiles and adjusts the beaded Indian headband that holds her hair in place.

"I'll straighten this out," I say. "Ha."

She giggles.

I giggle.

"I won't rape you," I swear, trying to conceal what promises to be a hard-on or an icicle, I know not which: my sexual disasters

7

of the past few months begin to fade from memory. For a wild moment I have hope.

So help me God I am sober and sane, she takes off her tattered mink coat.

And her tattered red sweatshirt with its motto: Whatsoever is Truth.

And her snowboots.

And her old-fashioned patriotic plaid skirt, the Maple Leaf tartan yet, one of the authorities observes.

And then she takes off her tits.

You heard me, Professor. Her sculpted and aerodynamic tits. And then she takes off her gold bracelet and her skirt-petticoat and her jockey shorts.

Maybe the cock and balls are fake too, I don't know. This is a peculiar land, Professor. Illusion is rife.

Two well-dressed Customs officials have been hanging around all this time and one of them finally says to me, "What're you waiting for, sir?" He picks up that pair of gorgeous tits and sticks his nose in between them.

And then he is all smiles.

I mean, all of a sudden you can smell the slightly green, the beautiful grass. I take a deep breath myself. The Customs man looks at the poor dumb bastard standing there in his earrings and his knee socks and his limp prick. "Next time you're waiting in an airport," he says, "remember to use the *ladies'* room."

But the fun has only begun.

"Get your pants off," the same authority says to me.

And then he's waving the Queen's Own flashlight up my Royal American.

"See anything?" the other one asks him.

"What do you expect," I venture wittily, bent over, "tonsils?"

"Say aaah," this other kid says.

8

They find nothing. I was robbed before leaving home. "There are trips and there are trips," my wife said, checking through my suitcase. The bitch kept everything for herself. "And I want you to get that job — so for God's sake go to the interview in your own head."

"Say ah yourself," an inquiring authority is saying to the kid.

"Aaaaoooooeeeeh," he says.

The authority who nearly lost a finger has another bright question. "Where've you been?"

"Mexico."

"Purpose of trip?"

"Bless you," the kid says. "I wanted to get some decent marijuana."

"Who owns these tits?"

"They are not mine, sir."

"Where were you born?"

The kid is standing there in his headband and his blond locks; the curly hair is his very own. "A difficult concept. In a previous existence I was a buffalo."

"You were a *buffalo*, were you?"

"In a previous existence. Now I am lost."

"You're going to find yourself, kid. In a room in the crowbar hotel. Get your panties — your shorts on."

The kid turns away to find his clothes.

He was once a buffalo. I admire that boy for his patience, for his tolerance of fools. I see that I have come to a new possibility. Be patient, I tell myself. Like that brave youth who was once a buffalo, out on these plains in a blizzard. Waiting out the storm. Enduring the bristle and blast of snow. The reaper's keen hook of the wind. Waiting out the winter.

This eight-foot Mountie appears out of nowhere and starts to lead my friend away.

9

"Hey," I yell. "What about me?"

"Wait," a Customs officer calls back, slamming a door in my face.

## 3

So have we all waited, Jeremy. Even the stay-at-home professors whom you would insult. So have I waited, if for nothing more than the end. Because at forty-seven one is weary of many things: the unfinished manuscript, thick and dusty on the corner of one's desk, under the pile of bills. The empty bed of one's bachelor-hood, smelling only of solitude. The rampant dreams of the igno-rant young. One is weary of the strident voice within; one is weary of the desire that will not let the exhausted body rest. I have loved too much. Too many. And to love is to wait.

Jeremy, out loud and at great length, clutching his micro-phone in his naked embrace, told himself to be patient. Patience, he tells himself. And why, he asks, does man venture into the unknown when he might be safe in his two-room walk-up apart-ment with beer in his refrigerator, spaghetti on his menu, unread books piled high on his bricks and boards, nooky in his sagging bed? The old conundrum, he tells himself, victim of his own rhetoric: the old shovelful of rice, he complains, but the bull's ass once again nowhere to be seen.

How nice for him, that he might think he was safe when at home. Let me only say, enigmatically, that I am safer in his bed than was he.

## 4

Professor, I've struck on an idea that is nothing short of inspired. Something you won't understand, granted the marvels of your logical mind. But I have to get out of this cubicle. I have to get to a telephone.

I climb into my woollen longjohns. I put on my faded blue denim shirt. I pull on my red lumberjack socks, my Levi's and my beaded moosehide moccasins with their felt innersoles.

Carefully I arrange my two braids, stretch the red woollen cap down to but not over my ears, give a tug to the tassel. And now I slip into my fringed buckskin jacket.

I've made a decision. I shall walk out of this place. I shall bravely, recklessly, escape from this suffocating dungeon: DIS-GUISED AS MYSELF.

I stuff my lined leather mitts into the pockets of my buckskin jacket and shoulder my trusty tape recorder. I pick up the suit-case, since it looks exactly like mine.

The door isn't locked. I open it. The corridor is completely deserted. I step out into the open, stride briskly towards the cor-ner that conceals a desk and a guard.

Every last person has disappeared. The desk is empty, cleared, abandoned. I feel panic, I wait; now I'm on an escalator. The escalator is empty but running. I ride to the second floor. Maybe this is the first floor; maybe I was in the basement. I look at the rows of empty easy chairs, the chrome and plastic chairs. The only action is in the orange drink container; this is where I eat. I stare at the Shadbolt painting of a labyrinthine airport . . . a labyrinth . . . I force myself into a telephone booth.

I forced myself in. I dropped the telephone receiver in trying to pick it up, fumbled two nickels into a slot. Once, years ago, briefly I possessed three buffalo nickels, all of them now lost. I lis-tened for the dial tone. I gave a low grunt. Something like a large, heavy animal pawing its way through a crust of snow. I felt better. Then I dared to speak. I spoke to an operator who at first couldn't hear me: "Hello. Hello? Hello —"

On the third try I had a voice that sounded exactly like mine. My confidence grew. I did not call the Chairman, Department of English, University of Alberta. After four tries I got the number of Mr. Roger Dorck, Barrister and Solicitor. Resident in a town called Notikeewin, which, I wouldn't be surprised, is a Cree word. Or a Blackfoot word.

Actually, I was given two numbers that I might call. Though I was assured there is only one Roger Dorck. When I dialed the second number I got an immediate answer.

A woman's voice ventured: "Yes?"

"Mrs. Dorck?"

I could hear that she was hesitating, was listening for me to go on.

"Mrs. Dorck?" I repeated.

"I am not — Mrs. Dorck."

"Is this his home?"

"No — This is not his house."

"Is Mr. Dorck in, please?"

"Mr. Dorck went across the line. On business."

"When do you expect him back?"

"He was due back tonight."

Her voice was pulled taut; she had been waiting for the phone, a message. And now she was waiting for me to speak. I must go on speaking, must find some strange and comforting words.

"I have his suitcase," I burst out.

I heard what sounded like a gasp.

"It isn't mine," I insisted.

She wouldn't speak. I found myself wondering, Have I enough change to pay for this call?

"I have his bag," I repeated.

"He phoned after, you know."

"Who phoned?"

"My husband. Robert. After he drowned."

And then, goddamnit all, she was crying. She was crying at the other end of the telephone line.

"Who are you?" she said. "What are you trying to tell me —"

## 5

Of course I have had to select from the tapes, in spite of Jeremy's instructions to the contrary: the mere onslaught of detail merely overwhelms. We grasp at something else.

And that something else is the professor's domain: the world of reflection, of understanding. The insight born of leisurely and loving meditation. The word made human. Jeremy, it would seem, only uttered a curse. The suffering woman reiterated her concern. Jeremy cursed again, his compulsion to speak become profanity, then hung up the phone. And so I am left with the unanswered questions: Jeremy's absolute fear of involvement set him to groping at his thigh for his microphone, even while the anonymous woman wept for her drowned husband who, as she would have it, telephoned after his drowning. And surely she saw an ominous parallel in the silence of her Mr. Dorck, the presumption of the vulgar Mr. Sadness.

Jeremy was confronting a transmutation of a kind he could not accept: he hung up the receiver and tumbled out of the booth and seized the suitcase that wasn't his, and he charged through the silence to find an exit.

He then presumes to describe for my edification that bleak and haunted landscape. The truth is, I was myself born out there on those wind-torn prairies, on the ripped edge of that northern forest — the details are unimportant. Perhaps I never mentioned as much to Jeremy. But no, he was the student, not I, and it was

I who set him his demanding task, his continent's interior to discover . . . I sent him out there as on a mission, as on a veritable
quest for something forever lost to me and yet recoverable to the
world. And he was — let me say it — failing. Failing miserably.


## 6

When I stepped from the air terminal, into the very midst of the
stars, the bus for the city either hadn't arrived or was long gone:
I saw a fellow climbing into an old car, taking care not to knock
a cowboy hat off his head. "You going into Edmonton?" I dared
to ask him.

He gave me a sly grin. "Not if I can help it."

"I beg your pardon?" I said.

"I'm heading *away* from Edmonton. Coulee Hill."

"That anywhere near Notikeewin?"

"We'll be going right smack through the center of that burg."

"Who's this 'we'?"

"You and me and this old crate. She'll make it. Throw your
bag in the back there on top of that saddle."

I didn't so much agree as obey. Nine years of graduate school
will do that for you. Listen. Jump. Like that time the dean found
me, Professor, pissing on a potted tree in the faculty lounge. Thank
God I was drunk. Like that time my old maid aunt caught me
measuring my prick in her clothes closet. With her tape measure.

"Giddyup."

The air is clean here. I mean, you can actually *see*. Even at
night, the shadows have stone edges. . . . And the Milky Way
made the snow-drifted wheatfields paler than snow, the shadow
of bush and granary blacker than black.

The driver, by deftly hitting a patch of ice, skidded around a
corner and onto a highway. He centered the car firmly in the

14

middle of the road and gave it rein; he ventured to converse.

"Got this trick knee," he said. "Sometimes I can't raise my foot off the gas pedal."

"That so?" I said.

"Damned weather makes it worse. This cold snap supposed to last?"

"Haven't heard the forecast," I said.

"She's a pisscutter for cold," he said. "But New York was no picnic either."

"New York, New York?" I inquired.

"I ride the rodeo circuit," my driver explained. "If you're going to die anyways, you might as well get paid for it."

Completely by accident he drove briefly on the right side of the road.

"Could we stop for a drink?" I suggested.

"Never touch it."

"I'm parched."

"Sunday. Everything along here is closed up tighter than a bull's ass in fly-time."

We streaked along that icy road, and I almost put my feet through the floor when a train ripped like a burst through our silence; it smashed into the silence behind us. Then there was only a snow fence beside the starlit tracks. And the tick, tick of the telegraph poles.

They made me notice the space — they or their shadows on the snow, on the horizon — and I couldn't even pretend to sleep. Because if I did I might wink out and be gone forever.

The bronc buster glanced aside for the third time to scrutinize at some length my moccasins. "You down from the North?" he wanted to know.

"Just visiting."

"Been south before?"

15

"I don't like to travel."

Off to my side of the car I could make out, dimly, one hundred miles of loneliness. Then we passed a farm where a yard light was shining high on a pole in a silent, empty yard, as if the farmer couldn't sleep without at least the comfort of that one small light. And I thought of Grey Owl's advice: if you get lost at night — stop; build a fire; wait for daylight.

We were doing something over eighty miles an hour.

The poplar groves, pencilled on the white fields, were only big enough to emphasize the emptiness. We glimpsed a feed lot, beside a barn, and maybe fifty head of cattle were huddled together to keep warm. If there was a house nearby it was lost in the snow: only a windmill showed itself, lifting its motionless wheel over the barn's roof.

"Muskrats," the driver said.

I looked at him.

He indicated a half circle of willows beside the road; he pointed towards, then looked back at, something he said was a frozen slough.

"Must make you lonesome," he added.

I grunted, trying to sound overcome by emotion.

"It must be a terrible chore," he went on, "to go around killing them by the hundreds in the spring hunt. Shooting and skinning."

I grunted again.

He seemed to remember something he'd forgotten; he began looking for it under the saddle on the back seat.

"Want me to take a spell at the wheel?" I said.

"Drive this road in my sleep," he assured me. He came up with a tin of tobacco.

"Can I help?" I said.

"At least," he said, "a bronc rider doesn't kill anybody but himself."

He began, with his right hand, to roll himself a cigarette.

"Let me help you," I said.

"Roll me a couple."

I pretended I hadn't heard.

And just as I was beginning to believe we were frozen into a kind of still but endless motion, a light blinked up on the horizon; then another; then what seemed to be a single flat row of lights that organized the star-glow of the sky.

That's when the driver said, "Notikeewin." As if by speaking the name he had created a place on the blank earth. I was moved. I was deeply moved by that one strange word, and I wanted my companion just to keep quiet and let me watch those lights turn into a town, into homes, into restaurants and streets and neon signs and movie houses. . . . I wasn't moved at all; I had been terrified, and now I was relieved.

"Where can I let you off?"

"Anywhere."

"No. I'm in no hurry."

And then, ten minutes later, the lights ahead of us were no closer. A new terror was settling into my bowels. I was seeing a mirage.

Off to our right the lights of another apparent town came, apparently, into view. I asked about them. The driver shook his head. "Never been there. That's thirty miles away."

"Notikeewin," the billboard read. "Population 8,421. Drive Carefully Please."

Just that suddenly I was thanking my generous host for the lift: I fell all over myself, being grateful. I couldn't shut my mouth. I was standing on the corner of an empty street, clutching a suitcase that wasn't mine. It was thirty-below or nothing, out there in that frigid night. I was alone in the middle of a strange town; not one human being was anywhere to be seen.

17

"My pleasure." The cowboy doffed his ten-gallon hat. I was scaring him; I saw that. "See you at the festival," he added.

## 7

Jeremy Sadness was a weird young tool, if ever God made one. And surely not the least of his peculiarities was a sexual anxiety that pervaded much of his behavior; arriving in the land of his imagination, he conceived the unlikely notion that his prick might freeze off. He walked through the midnight streets, the suitcase in one mittened hand, his balls in the other; and he might well have walked in circles until he stumbled, fell, and actually froze, had he not quite by accident rounded a corner and recognized ahead of him a railway station.

His first impulse, he claims, was to go buy a ticket so that he might get to his job interview on time. But just then, approaching the station, he noticed on his left, as if it had appeared only that instant, a statue of ice.

An Indian on a galloping horse bore down on a huge and galloping buffalo, leaned over both the buffalo and Jeremy, aimed an arrow of ice at their twinned hearts. Jeremy turned as if to dodge away. And he faced, on his right, a dogteam of ice; a trapper shaped from translucent ice was fixed into a slow trot behind an icy sled.

Blackfoot and Cree. Horse and dog. Imagine, Jeremy thought to himself, a pompous little impulse to theorize asserting itself, making beauty out of ice. The sun's bright hammer, coming down. The skull itself constricting.

He should have recorded a few insights for inclusion in his unfinished dissertation. Instead, he hunched warm inside his buckskin jacket; he went towards a banner that hung over the railway station; he spelled out to himself in the strange brightness of the night:

18

## 27th ANNUAL NOTIKEEWIN
## WINTER FESTIVAL
### February 3-4-5

That was four days away: by which time Jeremy was to be back in the classroom and teaching the medieval romance to his hairy class. In the lower right-hand corner of the banner was something in small print: he walked close enough to read:

### Winter King: Roger Dorck

I trust it would be fair to say that at that moment he abandoned all intention of showing up for the job interview.

The Royal Hotel across the street from the station was dark except for one dim light in the lobby. Jeremy awakened the clerk with his third tap on the desk bell. Ding ding. Or rather, he attracted the clerk's attention and persuaded him to sleep-walk; the clerk registered the traveller and led him up two flights of stairs and down a musty hall to a room without ever awakening.

### 8

I did not dream, Professor. My mind all night was space itself, undreamed, silence undreamed. Original. And don't ask me why, this morning when I peeked into the splotchy mirror over the basin in a corner of my room, I tried to reach through the glass and touch my own skin. And another temptation: I checked and found the tape recorder where I had left it on the night table. I wanted to turn it on and — no, not talk. Listen. I wanted to hear myself say I had landed safely, had not tumbled from the clouds, had not perished in a burst of exploding gasoline, of purifying fire. . . . I should have kept that tape I mailed you, you dumb-ox, Professor. Who are you, you pompous ass? Sitting there in your office in the Library Wing, chewing your cud, the grass you cropped off the green fields twenty years ago, vomiting it up into your own mouth, chewing it again. And again. Professor Madham, you did this. You sent me out here. You, with your goddamned go-get-a-job syndrome, publish, head a committee. Become a dean and die. Stick my unwritten dissertation —

I needed a toothbrush. I needed a razor. To have come thousands of miles, to have survived this far, the trials, the torments, and then to be marooned for want of a Gillette Blue Blade.

I couldn't open Dorck's suitcase. I couldn't bring myself to do it. *What if it contained my possessions?* So out into the street once more. And I'll be damned.

There, in the blinding snowlight of day, above the drugstore towards which I was headed, was a neat row of windows. And on the center window, in gold lettering the bald announcement:

ROGER DORCK
BARRISTER AND SOLICITOR

I climb against the long angle. I go up the creaking stairs to the "Don't Knock Enter" sign. And I do not knock.

Nor do I enter.

Somewhere a radio is playing country music and my ascent has not been signalled by the creaking stairs. Mr. Dorck, I see through the partially opened door, is not at the moment in his office.

A tall girl with her blonde hair flowing free. . . . Her hair is too young for her sombre face. An unsmiling woman, about the age and height of my own dark and sensuous Carol —

## 9

Yes, Miss Sunderman, this is the episode where he meets you. Lest he offend your feminine reticence, let me describe the event in my own words . . .

You are cocked forward over a desk on which lies open a suitcase, a Samsonite two-suiter. You touch the bone handle of the hunting knife: Jeremy used it to open letters. When he received letters. You laugh.

The laugh surprises Jeremy. He has already imagined you to be distant, a solitary of sorts, and yet a woman desiring her isolation to be violated.

You take hold of the red plastic handles of his grip developer. You squeeze. You laugh again. You hold up his underwear to the harsh light over the desk, contemplate the safety pin that supports the failing elastic. It is not a cruel laugh: and yet it cuts like an arrowhead clean through Jeremy. It leaves him, in a way that is vaguely sexual, immobilized.

Out of his suitcase, you are creating *him*. It is more than he can endure. You read the word TEMPLAR on two chewed pencils, then drop them and wipe the fingers of one hand with the fingers of the other. You frown, then smile, at the beaded Assiniboine headband. You try to smooth a wrinkled sweater, examine the leather patches on the elbows; you lift and let go of a blue denim shirt that needs ironing, deign not to touch a pair of socks out of which he hopes to get one more day's wear before surrendering them, as he would have it, to the soap merchants. He is sloppy, uptight, unclean: your version of a savage. Never once, not for a second, do you confuse him with Roger Dorck.

You open a new notebook to the first blank page, then notice he has brought along six of same, lest the dissertation should suddenly begin to write itself. A loafer. Not the ring-giver of old, not a leader of warriors, not a sound judge of good and evil. The eternal scrounging lazy unemployed bum of a graduate student —

You find the one notebook that is not quite new nor totally empty, raise it as if to close your — and here I quote — eloquent breasts therein: you bend your gaze to the first paragraph of the dissertation: "Christopher Columbus, not knowing that he had not come to the Indies, named the inhabitants of that new world —"

Then you read, aloud again, my own professorial comment: "Jeremy my boy, you have used this same opening in two other failed, futile, rejected attempts at writing a dissertation. When will you *begin?*"

You laugh. Jeremy claims to understand, for a moment, why the unbelieving are sometimes tortured, strangled, flayed, crucified, burned, or otherwise put to inconvenience. He knocks at the open door.

"Are you — Mrs. —"

"Mr. Dorck is not married."

And only then, moving away from the harsh light, do you really see him. He is not the friend you might have been expecting, not the admirer from down the hall who might share the immense joke that is the life on exhibit in that suitcase.

Jeremy is unshaven and wears no shirt over his bare chest. He has come in out of the icy sunlight in his levis and moccasins and his buckskin jacket. For your scalp. For your maidenhood. He reaches up with both hands and takes hold of his head, trying to straighten his tangle of black hair, his braids.

"Ha," he says. "Thank you."

"Is there someone you are looking for?"

You notice his jockey shorts spread out on the in-basket; and just for a moment an intimate smile plays over your mouth. But then you are serious again. "Is there someone you are looking for?" you repeat, as if you do not hear your own question.

"No," he bursts out. "Nothing. Yes, I am looking for nothing. The primal darkness. The purest light. For the first word. For the voice that spoke the first word. The inventor of zero."

God knows, he could be a pretentious little fucker, when he was rattled.

22

"Is this your suitcase?" you ask. Unexpectedly.

"Of course not. It isn't mine. Why do you ask?"

"You're here for the festival." You lower the notebook and put it down, open. "Which — Whom do you represent?"

"No one."

You fold the shorts and put them neatly into the suitcase. You might be packing to go on a vacation, you and Jeremy, an old couple taking the trip you promised yourselves in the flush of youth. Believing it will bring back the lost occasion. The pleasure spent or denied, dissolved in a blazing catastrophe.

"Just who on earth do you think you are?"

"Sadness."

"What about sadness?"

"No, no. Sadness. That's me. Jeremy Sadness."

You glance oddly at the notebook.

"Jill," you say. "Jill Sunderman."

"How do you do?" He takes your hand — he seizes your hand into his.

"When," he inquires, "will Mr. Dorck be back?"

"Then you haven't heard?"

He is silent. You retrieve your cool hand. You will not help him. You will not ever help.

"He was in that accident. Last night. On a snowmobile."

"No," Jeremy says. "He was flying last night."

"Yes," you say. "I met him at the airport. I dropped him here in time to lead a snowmobile trek."

"He had an accident," Jeremy says. As if he might be telling you.

"On his snowmobile." You reach out and he does not let you touch him. "They can't bring him to. The doctors can't bring him to."

It is the pain in your eyes that he cannot stand. No. The pain behind the control in your voice.

"Can you wait?" you ask him. "Until —"

23

"How," he demands, "did you get the suitcase open?"

"It was open when I got here this morning. Apparently some idiot took his bag." You indicate not the bag but the open notebook; the bold, unmistakable handwriting that asks: "When will you *begin?*" Your voice is rigidly controlled. "Look," you say, "Mr. Dorck must have read in this notebook, trying to discover who took his suitcase. And he printed across the bottom of the page: 'THIS, THEN, IS HOW IT ENDED.'"

You offer him the notebook so that he might see.

He turns away.

"Stay," you call. "Wait."

He stumbles off down the creaking stairs on the balls of his moccasined feet.

"They can't bring him *to*," you are calling above him.

### 10

Professor, I spent some money. Something you've probably never done. My wife's hard-earned pennies. The additional dollars borrowed, on the promise of an early death, from her father's oil-depletion allowance — after I merely crawled across the entire floor of his bank on my elbows and knees and kissed his fat ass. Endings be damned.

I bought a toothbrush. Then I bought a shaving set that was on sale, complete with a deodorant that is guaranteed to seal the body against disintegration. Then I ate two orders of pancakes in something called the Queen's Cafe. Then, recklessly, I found a men's shop: and I bought new socks, new shorts, a heavy sweater that I insisted on trying on over my hairy bare chest. I selected three red handkerchiefs. Don't ask me why: my suitcase is sitting there unclaimed in the office of Roger Dorck, Barrister and Solicitor. Winter King.

24

But I've lost my dissertation.

Even before I departed from my wife's last embrace I walked into the Xerox Room, hoping to run off a free copy of the opening of my potential masterpiece. Lest the original be destroyed in a two-plane crash or a bombing outrage. She was reading Hardy, my grieving spouse, for that course of yours, Madham, the one she's auditing for the third time.

"Excuse me," I say.

"What's bothering you," she says, "somebody offer you a job?"

"Miracles," I say. "You keep asking for miracles."

"Genius," she replies, "nine years is long enough even for *you* to be a graduate student; I'm sick of working day and night in this cheapskate fucking Xerox oven to keep you in beer money. But why should I rush home?"

It was too much. Granted, yes, I have my little hangups at the moment. But what am I supposed to do, slave away at a dissertation, teach two sections of Lit and Comp, review for a final oral, put up with the bull dyke who shares my office, grade fifty papers a week — and screw my horny wife on the hour?

## 11

Miss Sunderman, your year of birth is such that you are the same age as Jeremy's wife. Carol is a very attractive woman (widow?) of twenty-eight and, quite frankly, she has long been ready for a husband who is something more than a graduate assistant. I took her out to dinner on the day of Jeremy's departure; it was a Sunday, and what is there to do here in Binghamton after you've read the Sunday *Times*? We went to a motel-restaurant on the Vestal Parkway and made a pleasant evening of it, sipping cognac and even joking about Jeremy's endless excuses for not completing his degree requirements. Jeremy's own idea of a night out is spiedies

25

and beer in a seedy tavern, followed by steamed clams and more beer in another seedy tavern. When he has the money . . .

He went back to the hotel room from which he had issued and commenced his obscene little grip exercises, opening the closet door and squeezing one knob in each hand. Then he did his push-ups and his sit-ups and his running on the spot. After shaving and dressing he left his soiled shorts in the basin to soak; he slipped the strap of his tape recorder around his neck.

He went out into the street again, and followed ragtag after a crowd that led him to what was in fact the local curling rink. When he should have been engaged in his job interview, he was muttering pretentiously into his precious microphone, hunched fetally on a wooden bench, and once again avoiding what he claimed was the goal and purpose, the passionate intention, of his flighty quest. Avoiding life.

## 12

This is the kingdom of Dorck. Snow. And the cold sun. The curling rink one of his palaces: up the long ice the rocks ride smooth as a dream. And then they echo back the violence of their far encounters. Karoom. Karoom. Another figure bends here close before my eyes, one foot in the hack, one hand on the handle of the kettle-shaped chunk of granite: he reaches and lets go . . . the slow curling of the rock, as if it might be floating, drifting, disappearing far up the rink towards an escape I can't imagine . . . and then two sweepers bend before the slowing rock, burst into a furious dance.

Karoom —

Professor, this is serious. Roger Dorck is still out cold. I guess maybe I wish you were here: you would . . . well, this is silly . . . but at least you'd know what to *say*.

A hunting and fishing club — they all went trekking on their snowmobiles out along the rim of a deep valley that runs south and east from Notikeewin. On their way to a midnight supper in some little rural community hall.

Practice, it was supposed to be; for the festival contests. They came to the Lepage Ranch and stopped to have a drink with the lady who runs the place; they began to play games, racing and jumping with their machines.

The most skilled driver of all, Roger Dorck, went up and over a hump of snow, intending to make a leap the way those figures and machines leap on billboards. In the darkness, travelling fast, Dorck turned towards a hummock of ice and snow. And he leaped up and over; like a dream of himself he climbed, into the night air, free of the earth at last, his freed engine roaring —

But the hummock turned out to be a cliff that goes almost sheer into the valley of Wildfire Lake.

Roger Dorck began to fall; and then he was plunging, dropping free in the hard night air: and then he was sliding helplessly with his machine, over it, under it, skidding and tumbling in the drifts of suffocating snow towards a ravine's bottom and the first bluff of poplar and spruce.

And when four men got to him he was unconscious. When they lifted him onto another snowmobile he was unconscious. When they carried him into Our Lady of Sorrows Hospital in Notikeewin he was breathing, warm — but still as unconscious as when he was delivered from the slide of snow.

*Karoom.*

Already his leap is legend. In the curling rink the curlers speak only of their king; and they speak as if he vaulted the night itself, and only sleeps to restore his spending. The fucking fraud. I must see for myself —

*Karoom. Karoom.*

27

Pitiful, prying bastard that he was, our Jeremy. He went to the hospital, entered, talked his way past the sympathetic and unsuspecting nurse: so that he might view what he somehow conceived in his voyeuristic fantasy to be a living corpse.

He was in for something of a surprise.

The figure of Roger Dorck was in the room, to be sure. Jeremy stepped around the half-open door: and at first he saw only a pair of feet. For some reason they weren't covered: they must have held Jeremy's attention for a good thirty seconds. He noticed the untrimmed toenails, the blue veins, the fine red hairs on the long toes. All this he had time to remark before he saw the woman.

She was lying on the bed beside the comatose man. She had not heard the intruder enter the room and she lay silently at the side of the unwaking figure. Her sensuous mouth was seemingly pressed to his right ear.

Jeremy looked away from that unlikely posture. That Judas kiss.

Dorck was stretched out flat on his back, with not a mark on him to be seen. Not so much as a mark. Jeremy, being Jeremy, was disappointed. Dorck went on breathing with ease and regularity through his hatchet nose, over his thin line of red mustache; a tube of something or other ran from a suspended bottle into his right arm.

His hands, freckled, touched red with hair, were too big. They looked awkward; Jeremy had expected assured and meticulous hands. He was triggered into anger by that huge and awkward man, lying there so comfortable and at ease. He wanted to shout, "Get up, Dorck! People are worried about you. Show some consideration. Get your ass out of the sack."

And while he thought these things, Dorck slept on. A faint smile played over his face; or rather, a smile was fixed there stonily, never leaving, never changing. As if a Mayan statue had been made to smile.

The woman was making no sound. Unaware, she raised her right leg into such a position that Jeremy might see along her thigh. A crucifix on the wall gave assurance that, allowing for a few thorns and spikes and a little death, this might be the best of all possible worlds. Jeremy stared at those bare feet, up-ended, and so huge they seemed to leave a great portion of the world exposed. He looked again at the woman's thighs, the dark center of her crotch almost visible through her pantyhose.

He turned away and fled out into the labyrinthine halls. With his usual ease, he translated his basest impulse into a comment on the world's failure.

## 14

*Krankenhaus*, Professor. The world is a hospital. You better believe it, you with your bright-eyed love of the tragic figure. I walk the endless halls of this place: measles, hernias, cancer of the throat, ingrown toenails, leukemia, obstruction of the bowel, kidney trouble, knee trouble, ear trouble. I ask a man who is whimpering: "What can I do?" "Nothing," he says. I ask others, "What is it?" "Trouble," they say. Trouble. Always trouble. Stomach trouble. Heart trouble. Back trouble. "What's the trouble?" I say to an old man propped up in bed, staring ahead at nothing when I peek in at his door. "I can't breathe," he says.

And the insufferable silence. Talk. If they would just talk. The silence is worse than all the low, long sound of all the trouble.

It's a vigil, Professor. It is one son of a whore of a vigil at this unholy hour of the night. Over and over I meet this ancient nun who patrols the halls; she needs a shave worse than I do. I meet her and leave her and then I turn two corners and there she is again. Every time we meet she's praying and I'm muttering. This old nun nods and smiles and I go on muttering — to myself. She pops in on the rows of sufferers and whispers and consoles and coddles, she straightens a pillow and fills an empty glass with ice water. Sometimes a light comes on on a little board out in a hallway, and then it goes off, and another one comes on, and it goes off too, in a little while. My armpits are wet, under my buckskin jacket. Even the tin water jugs, they're sweating this one, I'll tell you. A nurse comes straight at me, around a corner, running as hard as she can without making any noise, as if she's invented a wonderful new dance; some poor devil needs a blood transfusion. Or an enema. Or a catheter. I make no effort to get out of her way.

I stray into the maternity ward: one whole glass room full of little babies either sleeping or crying. Sleeping or crying. There is no third possibility anywhere to be seen.

There is nowhere else to go. But back to the room from whence I came.

Roger Dorck is still on the verge of yielding to his own uneasy smile. Either he will scowl or break into a guilty grin.

That strange and beautiful woman lies undisturbed beside him, still seeming to whisper. She is kissing his ear or whispering. But what can she say? Roger, go back and take the other turn. Get dressed, Roger, this gentleman is taking us out for a drive. Stay home, Roger, stay indoors with your spaghetti and beer, read a book, avoid ladders. Let it go, Roger, jump, leap, fall, don't try to save anything . . .

She looks up at my watching. She smiles. Either at Dorck or at me. She nods. At which of us I can't say.

And now I see what she is doing. She is combing Roger Dorck's hair. Her hands, her healing hands, touch at the broken circle of his thick red hair. He looks as if he was scalped, then hauled in here alive and dead.

I want that woman. All of a sudden it is that simple: standing half-hidden by the half-open door I feel the first stirrings of an honest-to-God erection. Her pale and healing hands must touch me; I can only barely keep from flinging myself onto the bed. I could pitch old Roger out of his kingly silence, onto the floor. I could stretch out like a king myself, flat out and grinning from ear to ear.

"Will you see me home?" the woman is saying —

She is asking.

"Will you see me home?"


## 15

What follows comes very close to being the sort of deception that Jeremy's wife claims her husband was engaged in from the beginning. He simply does not give us adequate motivation, adequate *allowance*, for what happens. Intending to describe the woman, he says she is forty-five or so, a tall woman, proud and defiant in her grief — and then he breaks off and announces: This, Professor, is the woman you should have married.

Let me add one more detail.

The truth is, Jeremy was never much of a driver. Playing in what used to be one of La Guardia's playgrounds, there on Houston Street before it was widened, he had no need for an automobile. He learned to drive in the parking lots of SUNY Binghamton, in front of the women's gym, like a knight learning to joust.

The strange woman's car was parked in front of the hospital. Jeremy climbed in without speaking; he accepted the key and found the ignition switch. Grimly he drove north, into the center of Notikeewin, past the railway station, and on out of town. He drove, grimly, carefully, along a mile of deserted road. The barbed wire fence was barbed now with frost. The thin willow

31

posts managed to lift only the top wire out of the crust of snow. He came to a poplar grove where the snowplows had thrown the snow so high that he could not, for two hundred yards, see the reassuring lights of the town. Then, the town lost, he burst out into a space of wheatfields: their stubbles were drifted white under the fierce stars; the fences trailed off towards horizons beyond his seeing.

The Sunderman house is two of those tall, gaunt, weathered prairie houses pulled together, attached to each other, to make an awkward L. The double-roofed house is hardly to be seen, surrounded as it is by a dark grove of spruce, planted God knows when by a homesteader who couldn't stand the vision of space.

Jeremy followed the swerving trail in among the spruce. The woman indicated a turn to the left that would take them to a barn.

Just then, as he drove up to the open doorway, Jeremy saw in the glare from the headlights the white printing on the red wall of the barn, between two small hayloft doors.

He stopped and read again, straining to see, and he hadn't been wrong the first time: WORLDS END. Someone had left out the apostrophe. Jeremy drove in under the sign and turned off the engine.

The silence was absolute. He might have heard a mouse eating its way into a trunk in the attic of the house. In one of the attics.

But the woman was disappearing, leaving him alone, and he leaped out of the car. Jeremy claims he had no intention whatsoever of stopping. And he swears he wouldn't have, had not the northern lights just then flared red and green across the open sky above their heads. It was more than he could face: the sky consuming itself.

The interior of the house was an imprisoned garden. House plants of every ominous shade and shape crowded the windows, crept up and down the walls, hung in green tentacles from the ceilings. Begonias. Geraniums. Mistletoe cactus falling like chain from a brass pot. Philodendron reaching down from a basket. A spider plant complete with spiders. Potted palms. A rubber plant. A cut-leaf philodendron climbing a post. Ivy climbing up the railing of the stairs. The whole downstairs was a jungle through which at least two cats stalked each other. Or one cat played at catching itself.

The woman led Jeremy by the hand up a long flight of stairs. At the top of the stairs she took him into the north wing and down a long corridor to what seemed to be a bedroom.

To what might have been a bedroom. It was a long narrow room that contained, among other things, a large bed. But what it contained mostly was clocks. Two grand-daddies, one on either side of the head of the bed. Wall clocks with roman numerals on their faces. Arabic numerals. Calendar clocks that showed — that might have shown — the day and the date. Banjo clocks and lighthouse clocks. Lyre clocks and steeple clocks. Someone didn't trust the sun.

Or, as Jeremy put it, "This room looks more decadent than that old house of yours back there in Binghamton, Professor, where my wife loves to spend her free time rubbing and buffing."

And then he noticed something else.

Not one clock was ticking. Not one. Not one hand was moving.

He simply fell over onto the bed, exhausted; slowly he lifted one foot off the old quilt, while lying on his back, intending to unlace the first of his moccasins.

It was then she sat down beside him. She sat down and her long fingers touched his hands away from the moosehide thongs.

Jeremy waxes eloquent about what must be going on in the woman's mind. She is, he announces, at the core of her being, one of those listening women. She has been listening all her life, not just for a voice, the phone to ring. No, she has listened for a door to open among her plants and flowers, a stair to squeak. A twig to break in her private forest. The wind to rise. The snow to tap at the window.

In fact she was no doubt a little bit astonished at her own behavior, experiencing the lightest regret, and quite possibly already bored.

She had removed his moccasins.

And then she plunged. She took the leap into her own voice. Her own, if you will, silence. She was speaking.

"He phoned after, you know."

"Dorck?"

"No. My husband. After he drowned."

In all fairness I must report that Jeremy Sadness was for once in life surprised into a silence of his own.

"They never found the body, you know. Only the hockey stick, beside the hole in the ice. In spring, of course, the creek floods and they have to open the gates of the pond."

Jeremy was trying to speak, trying to break his jaws into motion.

"I started crying," she said.

"What could he possibly say?" Jeremy burst out. "What could a man say, phoning from —"

"And he hung up," she said.

"Listen —"

"He was hardly more than a boy. I had seduced him into marrying me." She stood up, face to face with a tall clock. "They had told him . . . he was the best hockey prospect they'd ever seen." She was speaking to the clock. "He had the perfect body," she added.

She admired him. By God that was obvious and certain: she admired Robert Sunderman for having the courage to leave. To knock a hole in the ice, fake his own death, and disappear. If he hadn't really drowned. If she was right about the phone call. And she went on admiring the sheer will power that had enabled him to stay away.

She sat down again. "I've never let Roger into this room."

Jeremy turned his face away from the light.

"He'll need the last sacrament," she added. "Extreme unction."

Jeremy signalled that he couldn't bear the light. She went to the switch by the door and touched it down. The slightest glow came in at the window; just enough to enable him to see the rococo pattern of frost on the pane, the new-made leaves and flowers of ice.

She was standing beside the bed. Jeremy was supposed to speak. He tried to raise a hand. It seemed a dead weight was fastened to his hand, and to raise one finger he must lift up from muck and clay the bed itself, the clocks, the room. To lift up a signalling hand he must lift up Carol, and me, and a suitcase that wasn't his, and four unfinished dissertations, and his mother, and poor old Dorck laid out cold in a warm and comforting bed. And the darkness itself.

And the next thing he knew he was dreaming.

Those chthonic plants came up the stairs. Tendril and leaf came curling down the long hallway and in at the door. Ivy and philodendron were binding him into the bed. He was rooted there, immobile. His breathing was as soft as the slow heaving of a hedge into spring. A spider tickled his nose. A crocus bloomed hairy and blue in his crotch. His feet were mossy stones. And yes, Robert Sunderman himself was due any moment, sliding as sudden as an owl, through the half-open door.

## 16

Bless me Father it is thirty degrees above zero in this sacristy: and my breath isn't the only thing that's freezing, let's make it fast. It is nine years since my last confession. The day I applied to graduate school. . . . I was an altar boy, in my youth, for Father Di Cesare at St. Anthony of Padua's. There on Sullivan Street, just off Houston. The church door itself just opposite our walk-up apartment; I could watch the virgins on their way to communion, tying on their kerchiefs, tugging their skirts. . . .

But to get to the point: last night, lying in bed in the home of the living wife of a man who might or might not be dead and gone, I was dead and gone. A total loss. I was afraid of ghosts, Father. AFRAID. While all the time I knew that in the next bedroom, downstairs, somewhere in one half of that double house —

Did you have full knowledge of what you were doing?

I was doing nothing.

Did you give your full consent?

I did. And still was doing nothing.

Was it a grievous matter, son?

It was a grievous matter. Nothing is grievous.

How many times, son?

Zero times zero. The square root of nought. My will come to nothing. The balding truth . . . Father, I want to lay it on the line —

Alone, my son?

Father, I've been having trouble for the past nine months, but now it's getting serious. Since I arrived here. Part of the PhD syndrome. It's a grievous matter.

Or with someone else?

Father, listen . . . I can't get a hard-on in bed.

Are you —

Listen to me, Father; I'm telling you something. I cannot get a bone-on *in bed.*

Are you sorry, my son?

Sorrow be damned, Father. Guilt. Old-fashioned guilt. Every

time I lie down I feel guilty because I'm not up and studying. Work on your new dissertation, Sadness. Review for the final oral. Retake that German exam. Write that paper that's four years overdue. I'M TOTALLY GUILTY.

Ten Hail Marys, my son, and ten Our Fathers.

Listen to me. It's a God's fact. My prick stands up. So I can't study. I go lie down. MY PRICK LIES DOWN.

And remember, son, you cannot receive communion if you have sinned against the Father. Now say a good act of contrition.

GODDAMN WILL YOU LISTEN TO ME. I lie down. Do you follow? With some graduate student chick big on D. H. Lawrence. Okay? An assistant professor's wife, crusading for liberation. I'm horny. See? Got it? My doodle is up. My drumstick. My hammer. My man-root. My tent-peg. My thumb of love. Like a howitzer. Like a thunderhead. So I lie down. AND DOWN IT GOES.

DOWN, Father. *Kerplunk. Crash.* Sympathetic magic. *Zonk.* Does a tree falling in the Sahara Desert make a noise? There are no trees in the Sahara Desert.

Did you have full knowledge of what you were doing?

No. Yes. Nothing. I WAS DOING NOTHING.

Did you give your full consent?

I TOOK AN OATH OF CHASTITY WHEN I WAS NINE YEARS OLD. STOP IT, MY AUNT SAID. STOP MEASURING YOUR PRICK IN MY CLOTHES CLOSET, WILL YOU? WITH MY TAPE MEASURE. AND GO WASH YOUR HANDS.

Was it a grievous matter, son —

## 17

Miss Sunderman, Jeremy was not aware that he had spent the night in your mother's house. He was not aware of her identity when she dropped him off, next morning, at the church, where he was to deliver a message to the priest. Your mother's passion to have Mr. Dorck dead and buried was overriding all other considerations: Jeremy himself was merely insensitive and didn't think to ask her her name.

The priest hadn't returned from the curling rink. All Jeremy had to do was explain briefly and succinctly that Roger Dorck, unconscious, unaware, out cold, was no doubt ready for the last sacrament. In the absence of the priest Jeremy resorted to his tape recorder and, in his fashion — if I might put it bluntly — used the microphone to masturbate.

Someone knocked at the door.

"Come in," Jeremy shouted.

No one came in.

He shouted again: "COME ON IN."

No response.

He strode across the room, knocked over a prie-dieu, and very nearly jerked the door off its hinges, experienced as he was at seizing doorknobs.

What he expected to find out there, I can't imagine. But he reports that he was surprised. He found himself facing a boy who might have been a cherub stepped down from one of the holy pictures above his head. Except that the youngster was missing an upper front tooth. That same boy gestured out towards the street, and Jeremy saw on his chest, on a red sweater, a winged head.

"We're supposed to take you. We've looked everywhere."

Jeremy replied that he'd been sitting on his ass freezing to death for an hour: an appropriate comment on his great western quest for manhood.

"Jill is waiting out here," the boy said. He gestured again with his bare right hand. "In the car."

Miss Sunderman, I played a bit of hockey out there myself. When I was a boy. Didn't we all? I know a boy's eagerness to get to the ice.

"I'm supposed to wait," Jeremy said.

The impatient lad didn't quite know what to say. He smiled his embarrassment. Then he remembered his missing tooth. "Knocked out," he volunteered. "Last year at the festival. We were in the play-offs —" He touched a large, padded glove to where the tooth had been.

Jeremy raves on, comparing the tooth's absence to a sabre scar, a tattoo, a scarlet plume. In fact it was merely part of the game to lose a tooth or two: even now I wear a bridge where my right eye-tooth used to be. And Carol will sometimes fondly run her tongue over the solid gold, teasing in her youthful way about my past exploits.

Jeremy, of course, was always the student: he saw in the young face great portents: the child-player was destined to grow up and travel east to play left-wing for the Boston Bruins, for the New York Rangers. Seeking fame and money and easy women. And Jeremy wanted to warn him: it was the missing tooth that did it. The jawbone scar. The scar that was not guilt and pain but innocence restored, made bedrock strong. Never leave. Don't go. Stay home.

They climbed into the back seat of the car, the boy and Jeremy together; the boy took off his overshoes and began putting on his skates while you, Miss Sunderman, drove into the center of town, past three grain elevators, along the railway tracks and westward past the station . . . towards Elkhart Pond and the place where your father drowned. At least that is how Jeremy reported the event: you might want to square his account with your own recollection.

Jeremy, as you may have noticed, told the boy nothing.

Elkhart Pond, as Jeremy describes it, is a huge sheet of ice in the northwest quadrant of Notikeewin; you drove him out to the frozen pond in Dorck's big car and stopped on the shore by the almost completed ice fort; you faced, across the ice, a rather steep hillside. On top of the rise are the skating arena and the curling rink and the ski jump. Jeremy entered Notikeewin from that side of town.

You reached and turned the radio low, and were almost lost in the din of the snowmobiles' engines. Six machines, in motion, were trying to form a starting line. The driver of the outside machine, noticing the car, swung away from the competition, came scooting towards you like a bullet.

"This kind gentleman," you explained to Jeremy, "has agreed to take you for a ride on a snowmobile. If you're going to judge —"

"*Judge,*" Jeremy bellowed. "Who the — What the hell am I going to —"

"We'll give you a choice. Don't worry."

"No," he said. "Never. That's final."

"We're short of experienced judges," you said. "Everyone here is partisan."

"So am I," he said.

"Then whom do you favor?"

"The goof-offs. The self-deceiving inept. The honest inept. The conniving idlers. The reckless blowhards rightly and justly proud before an undeserved fall. The born and contented losers. The moderately depraved. The runaway survivors."

Our hero was not in an easy frame of mind. You opened the glove compartment of Mr. Dorck's car; you brought out a starting gun and pushed it at him barrel first.

A crouched figure was watching through a woollen face

mask. Its eyes were blue inside a set of blue and yellow circles. Its mouth was being devoured inside another red and frosted mouth. The strange face waited inhuman outside the window.

Meekly, Jeremy surrendered his tape recorder into your lap. He refused the gun.

## 19

Going around the half-mile circle, me hanging on to that stranger as if he was my soul, I began at first simply to relax. The wind, the noise, tore at us. But I felt pretty good: the cold at first was exhilarating. I gave a whoop and a shout. That great machine between my legs responded by surging forward. I shouted again. Yes sir, I was beginning to understand why Dorck went out to the edge of a cliff and took a crack at flying. The earth was too small. I wanted the sky as well.

But my face was beginning to stiffen. And we didn't show any signs of being ready to stop. My cheeks went raw; then all feeling was gone. Behind the inadequate skin was a nail-pierced forehead that ached with cold. My eyes, in their frozen tears, could no longer turn. I turned my head as an owl turns. My arms were steel traps that held me onto that mechanical devil. My outspread knees were becoming rigid wings of bone and cloth. I longed for the sun.

And then I was flying. All by myself I was sitting up there in the air, floating free. It seemed to last for a long time, that flight. I thought about Jill; I hoped she was watching, impressed. My ass was no longer being jolted.

And then I was driven like a post into a snowbank. That wasn't so bad either. Under the crust of snow I was out of the wind. I felt very comfortable. The world was liquid again; I was drowning in snow that yielded to my arms, closed over my head.

I made no effort to stroke my way back to the surface. I gave up the ghost.

But some idiot took me by the heels and pulled me back into the blinding light. Six people were dusting me off, looking frantically for injuries.

Not a scratch. Not so much as a scratch.

"You want to drive back to the car?" the kind gentleman in the mask wanted to know, kicking a roar out of his machine. Offering me his mount.

"I'll walk," I signalled. With a shake of my head.

That's when I discovered I couldn't take a step. I was rigid with cold. My arms were fixed at my sides, my legs were fixed, rooted in the loose snow. Snow on my eyelashes told me that I was inside a snowman, looking out on a strange, distant world. Then someone gave me a tug; somewhere below me a foot appeared and moved forward, saved me from falling. A second foot appeared and placed itself ahead of the first, as if the two of them had entered into a hopeless competition that was to carry me careening, jolted, weary, aching across a South Pole of ice. Scott of the Antarctic, I thought to myself, inside your frail web of veins and arteries, the center of warmth grows smaller. You are right to make the last entry and close the notebook, let the pencil slip from your hand. You have only to listen now. Say no more. Listen to the fall of silence, hear your own last breath and know for one instant you are no longer. After the long walk, the final pleasure; the surrender that is as good as, better than, the infinite struggle . . .

## 20

You helped him into the car, Miss Sunderman; you pulled off his mitts, began to rub at his knuckles. You took his left hand in yours, raised it to your mouth, to the warmth of your breath. You were, for some generous if misplaced reason, resolved that he should live.

And then, worse than the freezing, came the thawing out.

The needles in his flesh, in his face, his ears, stung at first as welcome evidence that he had, temporarily at least, survived. But they did not stop at the reassurance of warmth. The stinging needles turned fire red. The joints of his legs were needle-touched, then flame-tormented. His fists ached themselves into a life more numbing than frost. His heels were pierced.

Your hands dared to console him. Perhaps he faked some of his pain, for that very reason. Gently, gently, you touched at his flaming ears. You snuffed the fire of his nose. The frost on his eyes was steaming away; you touched him into seeing.

And then you kissed him. His unfeeling cheek. Why you would kiss a pillar of ice, one hesitates to guess. And your white hands touched his failed knees.

You would create him into life. Into his own life. He drove a wooden fist between his thighs.

No feeling whatsoever. He seized his own apparatus. He might have been seizing the neck of a decapitated chicken. Gone. The very last sensation, vanished. Even Roger Dorck, unconscious, could get from the unconscious ebb and flow of his blood, an erection. Not so Jeremy.

He groaned aloud.

Your hand descended onto his fist. "Are you all right?"

"No," he groaned, just able to chatter one word out of his blue mouth.

"Don't worry," you said. Unawares, you were resting your innocent white hand where his failed *cock* — I use his expression — might have been. "I'll take you out to World's End."

"World's End," he whined, incredulous even in the face of a simple truth.

43

"My mother's place —"

He groaned as he had not groaned before. "That beautiful, fated, *fortunate* woman —"

"Bea Sunderman. You've gone and met my mother —"

"Ha," he interrupted.

And then he imposes on the defenseless Mr. Dorck a motive and an intent that were surely his own.

"Dorck, " he fairly shouted. "Your mother *was* his mistress. Now —"

You nodded your head. Then you shook your head, Jill. That's all Jeremy tells us. Did he *forget* something? Why did you not smash him over the rooted source of his greasy braids with his own tape recorder?

He lowered his voice. "He likes you."

"Yes."

"He proposed."

"Yes."

"You turned him down."

"Not exactly."

"You accepted."

"Not exactly." Again, you shook your head. "Sunday night. After he got back. I need to talk —"

"I know a man like that," Jeremy said. "The shithead fawns after innocent women —"

"No." You turned sharply to face him. "Don't you see? I thought of him as a *father*."

At that moment he had, at last, an insight: which he immediately attached to poor Dorck. That sleeping man was charged with nakedly lusting after both: both mother and daughter. The ice of the daughter's concupiscence. The mother's nihilistic surrender. Now Jeremy recognized the terror of Dorck's night. The leaping night. The falling night. No wonder Roger fled his own return. Bitter and bleak, the dream. To embrace in each the memory of the other. The naked pleasure of complicity and violated love, the trust betrayed and cemented, the desire reminding desire, the older lust made new again, the new lust old and wise. The cry repeating the cry. The secret rage to fuck the healing mother of death, the virgin stark. The flesh of flesh renewing the flesh. The bush of the mother's bush.

"I have an idea," you whispered. You must have read his mind.

He picked up the starting gun as if he would contrive to blow out his brains.

"Thursday night," you were saying — he thought it must be some sort of lewd proposition — "Roger was supposed to judge. But you can do it instead. You can choose the festival queen. The *winter queen.*"

And then you burst out laughing.

You knocked a hole in the ice with your laugh. He leaped. He plunged in at the broken edge. Returned, returned. Into the bath of cold, and down. The white world around him turning black. Your laugh, he claimed, he raved, was that of some odd creature come to ravish the frozen earth: you are of the north, cold, blank, oblivious, whimsical, murderous, amoral, stark. The stark, amoral virgin.

"I have one question," he chattered.

You touched your hand closer. To his disaster.

"Where is the bus depot in this goddamned town?"

You took the gun out of his hand. You lifted the strap of his tape recorder onto his aching shoulder.

## 21

Professor Madham, I believe I called you a shithead of the first order; forgive me. Let me apologize again. At the next meeting of the Friday Night Mead Sippers, please extend my apologies as far even as the members of the faculty who know you best. Raise high the hydromel. Your judgment is sound, I perceive that now. Tell Newman. Tell Norcross. Tell Leranbaum. Tell Dykstra. Tell Speckman. Tell Levy.

I'm grateful to you for using your pull to get me this interview, jobs are scarce. Carol wants to have a baby soon; we should own a car; maybe we can borrow enough money from her parents to make a down payment on a house. I'm sorry I went charging off in the wrong direction when I got here —

Miss Jill Sunderman drove me to the bus depot in Noti-keewin. Last night. She works here in Edmonton, except when it's festival time; then she takes her vacation. She lent me the key to her apartment, so I might get myself together and make a phone call or two, explaining the appointment I missed.

And I should phone home, I realize that. Damn the expense. I was anticipated in Binghamton today, I believe, the victorious hero returned with tales of interviewers falling into spellbound silence. I should do it, Proffo, I should definitely phone. But I've been sitting here most of the day reading old copies of *Time*, doing my grip exercises; I keep hearing the conversation before I have it and then I can't dial:

Hello dearest Carol my love my all.

Who is this please?

Your devoted —

I've warned you that I notified the police.

No, no, it's me. Your own precious Sadness.

Hello, Jeremy, why don't you identify yourself when you call; you know I hate people who don't identify themselves.

It's me, you know who I am. Remember? Are there any messages for Mr. VIP?

Messages?

Messages. Communications. I've been gone.

Oh. You've been away, Jeremy. Of course. Your so-called mistress phoned.

She's worried about me.

She's worried about herself. She thinks she's pregnant.

You know, dear, underneath all that nastiness, you're something of a bitch.

That undergraduate you've been screwing in your office. I say, she thinks she's pregnant.

Doesn't she know the New York abortion laws? What's that damned university teaching her?

Money, Jeremy. Money. Abortions cost money. We borrowed heavily from my father so you might avoid work for nine years. So you might go well-heeled to your job interview. Would it really be polite to touch him for an abortion as well?

The horse's ass is as stupid as an ox and still he manages to stay rich. I'll be more careful.

Why not just get a job, Jeremy? If you don't *fuck* any more successfully than you seek gainful employment, then I can't begin to understand why Miss Cohen thinks she's up the flue. God knows, I'm in no danger of getting pregnant by you. But I suppose there's the complication of my job —

Carol, just as soon as I graduate. The minute I get this dissertation out of the way, get situated, pay a few debts —

Miss Cohen says you talked to her about running off to Europe together. Greece. Mallorca. Greece is a dictatorship, Sadness —

I can't do it, Professor. I can't phone. The great god Tit has got me confused with somebody else. Who is Tit? You tit, Tit. Carol, I'm sorry. No. Professor. Listen. Me with my genuine nose for calamity, I keep mistaking appearances for joy. This Miss Cohen.

47

It started quite by accident. Let's make love up against the book-case, I suggested. Are you *kidding?* she said. So I slipped it into her right there, Lit and Comp 1, Section 13, tits on her like snow-capped volcanoes: we were in my office in the Library Tower. She wanted to know about passion. What is a destructive passion, Mr. Sadness? she inquired. My office looked like a barbershop after, there were pubic hairs scattered from my *Norton Anthology* through *Anatomy of Criticism* to my notes on Bishop Berkeley (thus I refute the Bishop). My goddamned tile floor looked like a barbershop on a Saturday afternoon, I mean we really went at it propped up against the bookcase, then the windowsill, then the splintered edge of one of those decrepit hazardous desks they fob off onto graduate assistants. Her left foot up on my swivel chair. When are you supposed to menstruate? I kept asking her; and then I was down on my knees with a wet paper towel mopping up the scattered hairs, it was like trying to wipe out traces of a forest fire. And in walks my office mate, this decadent virgin bull dyke from Long Island they've quartered on me.

"What's the trouble, Sadness?" she wants to know.

"Spilled my hair lotion," I tell her.

Reggie. Fresh back from an invigorating half hour with her analyst. "I went to the City to see my analyst," she reports. Again. Miss Cohen is engrossed in a recent issue of *Notes and Queries.* She eases herself gingerly down onto a corner of Reggie's desk. "The local shrink isn't as smart as I am," Reggie explains. I say nothing. "I think a lot," Reggie says. "It's very fascinating, human nature is just fascinating." I'm standing up now, with my back to Miss Cohen, who runs a delicate hand up my spine. My shirttail is out, I forgot to tuck my shirt in. "I think a lot," Reggie continues. "Things keep making a lot of sense." Miss Cohen, quietly, unobtrusively, raises one soft gentle knee into the crack of my ass.

Reggie reaches for a chocolate.

Professor, you son of a bitch, you assigned that raving monstrosity to my office. To persecute me. To spy. To make me feel guilty.

I was getting a hard-on again. At my best I was phenomenal. "Miss Cohen," I said, "why don't you run along to the Rare Book Room?"

She doesn't move. No. She moves her knee again.

Hello? Carol? I see it now. I apologize. I was wrong. I'm guilty. Right. Your favorite professor drove me to it. By putting that goddamned Reggie in an office with me; she studies twenty-four hours a day. No wonder, who would screw her? And yet she has time to organize EGO. English Graduate Organization. Magnificent. She's at my ear day and night ordering me to defy the tyrants, which means, I take it, that I'm supposed to assault her maidenhead. I can't do it. I haven't been trained. Literary Methods 301 wasn't adequate to the task. A pretty girl comes into my office and Reggie beats me to her. Three years of squatting in a telephone booth with that intellectual giant, thank God she's ready to graduate. We sit back to back in that goddamned little hole of Calcutta doing our German grammar, and hour after hour I hear her swallowing chocolates one at a gulp. Something like ninety-nine beautiful sex-starved females in that department and I've got to share an office with the chocolate monster. Mary Shelley, you've done it again. That anonymous letter I got threatening to expose me to the Vice-President for Academic Affairs. *She* wrote it. She wrote it, the goddamned thing smelled of cheap chocolate, and then she sat there watching me sweat for two weeks. Was it a joke or wasn't it a joke? How do you tell in this world? After the first time with Miss Cohen. Read this for me, will you, Jeremy? One thousand words of plagiarism. What do you think, Jeremy, A? Or B-plus? Pretty soon I'm grading half her papers for her. On top of my own. Then I'm grading every-thing in my whole life: lunch at McDonald's, C-minus; my wife's spaghetti, F; Miss Cohen's swollen nipples, A-plus; The Defeca-tion in Swift Man lecturing on sin, C over D; the cheeks of Miss Cohen's perfect ass, A-plus; a memo from the Acting-President on turning out lights, A-minus; my brilliant little lecture on *Hamlet*, F; Miss Cohen slipping her panties into my desk drawer lest we be surprised of a sudden, A; my Xeroxed letter applying around the nation and into foreign lands for gainful employment, F-minus; Miss Cohen straddling my lap on my broken office chair (yes, I could and probably still can make it sitting even if not lying), A-plus; my three job interviews at MLA, F-minus; my friendly explanation to my professor, my wife, my father-in-law, my dissertation committee, my dead mother, my draft board, my unremembered father, my bank, my mother-in-law, my anti-scientific aunt, Matthew Arnold, Grey Owl, Our Dean who art on the fifteenth floor hallowed be Thy Keyholes . . . F F F F F F F F F F F F.

A failure. An F-minus-minus-minus fucking failure.

But straight-A Reggie never falters. Never misses a stroke. The faithful finger. She uses my notes, my books, my pencils, my typewriter, my stolen paper. She eats half my lunch when my wife is considerate enough to make me a lunch. When I'm sick or hungover she takes my goddamned piddling little class at a minute's notice and waddles in there and bangs out her brilliant canned lecture on capital L Literature that leaves me looking like a tongue-tied idiot. And all she wants in return is my cock. Yes, my cock. The only woman in creation I COULD NOT SCREW UNDER ANY CONDITIONS WHATSOEVER: and I'm locked up in a cage with her for sixteen hours a day. She can't get up from her chair and squeeze past me to take a piss without rubbing twenty pounds of tit up against the back of my skull. Or her biggest thrill: to sit in our broken-down easy chair with her bare feet up around her neck: for the first six months in that office I thought she was wearing a full beard.

Poetry. It's the mainstay of life. But goddamnit, why does she get all the fellowships? I get the extra section of Lit and Comp. I stagger in from grading two thousand freshman themes on what God means to me, and she sits there on her fat can telling me we should organize. What the hell does she know about it? Her idea of a benefit: a lifetime subscription to *PMLA*. Vibrators in the ladies' room. Free chocolates.

Oh yeah, Dr. Tragic Vision in Modern Prose: while we're examining my insatiable need for total failure. What about your own goddamned masterpiece, fifteen years in the burgeoning? Two sabbaticals and one leave of absence. Three summers in the south of France. Four trips to the British Museum. Fulbright in Athens. Guggenheim in Rome. Nine incidental grants-in-aid for miscellaneous expenses. The unpublished, unwritten, ill-conceived definitive study of nausea. I don't expect to read the brilliant opening chapter in my lifetime. But when do we get to see the Preface? When do we discover that this is to thank Professors Grunt and Fart for drinking stout with me in London? This is to thank Aristotle for his timely observations on the modern novel. This is to thank my students for doing my research. This is to thank Mrs. Jeremy Sadness for looking enthralled while I blather. This is to thank the departmental secretaries for writing the book.

And another thing. Why *are* you a bachelor at 47? You're handsome enough to deceive a literate woman. Show them your great collection of antiques. You must have money, God knows you don't cross the street without a national fellowship to cover the costs of transportation. Why always squire married women to the quartet concerts when you could be making it — With the girls in the typing pool. With the phys. ed. ladies. With the liberation mob. With the women higher up in administration.

Professor, I know your type. I know why my wife gets the hots for you. Jeremy, she says to me, you're so gross, so *physical*. And I know what she's thinking. If only you were like Dr. Madham, Jeremy. If only you were wise and insinuating and grey at the temples. If only you were a mind-fucker, Jeremy. Because that's what I need. Oh God, that's what I need, I don't need a beast like Jeremy Sadness. I don't need you with your clumsy rutting, I need a man like your professor. I need a man who transcends, transcends. I need a transcendent man, Jeremy. I need a MIND-FUCKER.

Hello, hello, Professor? I didn't mean to wake you up. Ha. Are you still there? Well listen to me, baby, now it's my turn. Finger your grade book nervously.

I've been hiding here one whole damned day in this apartment. I can report that the sun comes up and then goes down. Nothing to be sneezed at. A short day, covered in snow. Night approaches. I've read not only all of Miss Sunderman's magazines but also her cereal boxes, her jam jars (this is a bilingual nation, Professor), her bread wrappers. She has all these goddamned books in a great big bookcase: I'm too nervous to read a book. And no TV. And I've eaten her out of house and home: at the moment I'm down to a half-box of oatmeal cookies. So, after devouring all the food, I have to do my exercises. I've exercised for four hours today. Two hundred and six sit-ups. Three hundred and fourteen push-ups, though sometimes with my fat gut remaining immobile on the carpet. Running on the spot until the sweat rolls down the crack of my ass like the Susquehanna in full flood. And then when I'm too exhausted to stand, I sit down and work on my grip. I squeeze raw potatoes.

Yes, I am reluctant to go outside. Quite right. Don't know

whether to shit or go blind. Right again. But I'll show you how to dial a telephone. Alberta Government Telephones, it says: In Case of Fire. . . . If that vanished boy-husband-father could telephone Mrs. Sunderman from the watery grave, at least I can stick my finger in this hole. This hollow eye of the octopus . . .

"Balding? . . . Oh hello Mr. Balding. This is . . . this . . . Sadness. . . . Yes, Jeremy Sadness. . . . No, no, I'm calling from New York. . . . I seem to have misunderstood. Good grief, sir, I thought I was to see you *Thursday*. . . . *Monday*, you say. My mistake. My apologies, sir. . . . Yes, I'll be flying out tonight. Don't bother meeting me at the airport, I'll be late. . . . First thing tomorrow . . . yes, sir, 9:30 on the button, I'll be pounding on your door. . . . Ha. . . . Right. . . . Yes . . . no, perhaps my dossier didn't make it absolutely clear, the dissertation isn't *quite* finished: a matter of a few days at most, a footnote here, a correction there . . . yes, yes, family problems. I don't mean to make excuses, sir; let the chips fall. . . . My university of course has its own press, does some excellent bindings. Is it true that you're working on a definitive. . . . Oh. Thank *you*, sir. . . . Yes. Right. . . . Yes, I'm looking forward to it too, sir.

### 22

Miss Sunderman, I include the following passage or two from the tapes, not to embarrass you, rather that you might comprehend Jeremy's indecent concept of his own staggering charm. I know you would not have surrendered your honor so whimsically to one so crude, even perverted.

The forest of my own intent is inhabited by strange creatures, surely. The figure of Roger Dorck for one comes to haunt me. He was a dedicated man who spent his life caring for the family of a drowned friend. I cannot for a moment accept the notion that his "accident" was motivated by disappointment in love. Accident is a part of our daily lives; if not, then all of modern physics is madness. Are not explanations themselves assigned almost at random?

Consider Jeremy's attempts to explain his own irrational need to seek out the wilderness. He blamed much of it on the accident of his name: that one portion of identity which is at once so totally invented and so totally real.

He insisted again and again that he was only nine years of age when he walked up to 42nd Street one afternoon to find a book on Jeremy Bentham, philosopher and jurist: and found instead a photograph of a dead man, his body manicured and dusted, his head of wax wearing curls and a broad-brimmed hat, his skull on the floor between his feet. All of him attired in his accustomed clothes. That hero of our reasonable world had ordered himself stuffed and embalmed: he had become his own icon, sitting in a chair in a fine display case. In University College. At the foot of the stairs.

The frightened boy went racing home to his mother.

"Your father," she explained, "after he came to the hospital and saw you lying at my breast, named you Jeremy Bentham. He walked out of the hospital and came here for his suitcase and I never saw him again."

She was busy, as she told him this, ironing trousers for the tailor who lived across the hall on the fifth floor of that tenement building. The little tailor who so often came to Jeremy's mother's apartment, and who sometimes lent him the books of Grey Owl. "He wanted you to grow up," she added, "to be a professor."

"Wasn't my father —" the boy began to ask.

"He was only a sailor," she said. "After he disappeared, I don't know what he did. I once received a postcard from Genoa, and sometimes I think it was from him. But it wasn't signed."

He could ask no more; the little tailor was standing in the doorway.

"Come in," the boy said.


## 23

Professor, I stuck out my tongue at myself, in front of the hall mirror; I thought I might be getting sick. I stripped off my clothes onto a heap in the middle of the living room floor and I leaned against the large bookcase, studying titles. *Wanderings of an Artist. The Double Hook. A Jest of God.* A quick review, so that I might indicate to Mr. Balding I had not wasted a moment's time. But I found myself thinking of Miss Cohen — deliberately, desperately, I thought of her, hoping thereby to shut from my mind the indecision as to whether I should telephone Jill. Or Bea. Or Jill. And I remembered the slow, sliding journey from Miss Cohen's swollen left nipple to her swollen right nipple, down her slim body to the perfect circle of her belly button, down to the first fringe of tickly hairs . . .

Down all right.

Turning my head, I happened to see my reflection in the many windows. My decapitated body hung in suspension in the night air fifteen floors above the sidewalk. It was unbearable. I had, quite frankly, anticipated the simple pleasures of once again wacking my duff. Pounding my pud. Once again, in vain. I seized a raw potato and squeezed it six times. I fell to the carpet and did ten push-ups. I went to the windows and exhibited my failure from the bright aluminum casements of the Klondike Towers. My gross and absolute failure. I opened a window: the healing blast of icy air, the shrivelling blast that staunched the blood. . . . A study in decline. The skull itself constricting. The ultimate snowman.

I attempted to flog my limp imagination.

As far as the eye can see the bedrooms are stacked in columns and towers. And all the hard winter long a festival of desire crackles on Edmonton's metallic air: the whole night is a cold, electric blue. Like winter lightning, yes. People in love making love in bed. And far beyond the city's sensual iciness is the blackest black horizon I have ever seen, one huge rim and circle of pitch-black mystery. Edmonton the Gateway. The Gateway North . . .

No. It was no use.

I retreated into the john to escape the many windows. Chance and misfortune compelled me to borrow a toothbrush, paste and a razor from Miss Jill Sunderman's medicine cabinet. If I could not be dirty, then I would be clean. I was in a tub full of suds and hot water, almost asleep and slipping under, when I heard the hall door creak.

The hall door opened.

Footsteps came ghostly across the living room floor; stopped where my clothes lay in a heap. Continued.

I might have been caught adrift in a rudderless boat by a sudden hurricane. The water lapped at my ears, whispered at my ears.

"Anybody home?" a voice called.

"Help," I whispered. "I'm drowning."

Jill Sunderman came to the bathroom door, walked in as Carol might while I'm trimming my toenails. The walls of the bathroom are too white, the overhead light too strong. I couldn't look up.

"What's the matter?" I said. "What're you doing here?" She sat down on the toilet lid. "It's my apartment. Remember?"

"What's up?" I insisted. "The festival —?"

"I have to be back in the morning."

And then I noticed for the first time: she was beyond all her own gift of laughter.

"Hey," I said. "What gives?"

She was sitting there on the lid of the toilet in her heavy coat, proper and stiff and almost terrified. And carefully she recited in an I've-been-rehearsing-all-day voice: "I suppose I want to go to bed with you."

Somewhere deep in the deep, warm water I slipped; my face went down, under, the suds closed over me; then I re-emerged, unable to open my eyes. I groped with one hand to find a towel.

"Get your clothes off," I said. "Come into the tub."

"There's a perfectly good bed in the next room."

"I'm a virgin," I insisted.

"You are like hell," she said. "You're probably married."

"I took an oath not to screw until my dissertation is submitted for binding."

She tried to laugh. Jill tried to laugh.

I opened my eyes. Jill Sunderman reached over, put her hand on my face, pushed me under the water again. I tried to rise up. She didn't let me. For a frightening moment I thought she was serious. Gifted graduate student found drowned in bathtub in high-rise apartment, promising career cut off abruptly. Wife flies in from Binghamton, New York, to identify remains: refuses to claim same. Pauper's grave is now being dug in snowbank . . .

I caught at Jill's wrist, came up gasping.

"Third time down is for keeps," she was telling me.

I managed to force my eyes open and I glanced along the surface of the water. My prick was afloat in the suds like a strand of seaweed, rudely afloat on the sloshing waves. Drown, I said to myself. Drown, you useless prick. I raised a wet arm and banged an open palm against the side of the tub, splashing water up and between Jill's bent knees. "Push me," I pleaded.

I rose, stood up, dripping, from the warm water. I believe I expected Jill Sunderman to start up in terror and flee. She reached over, calmly, and took hold of a large towel. By God, she'd rehearsed it; she'd rehearsed the whole scene, right down to cradling my balls in a warm towel. She took hold of me.

I was standing up. I resorted to the ultimate goddamned onanistic fantasy: I imagined my wife. I imagined Carol in her home; we were single then, in the bedroom next to her parents'; Carol dropped her panties to the floor; I snatched them up as if the very crash and boom of their falling must raise the restless mother —

But we'd had a bad scene before I left. Carol and I. The last night, the tender moment before I ventured into the world to seek my fortune. We were in the sack. "Read," I said. She pulled a book off an unpainted plank, dusted it; she began to read: Gibbon, *The Rise and the Fall*. No, *The Decline and Fall* . . . history of same. "I don't like it," she said. "No," I said, "read. Read on." Maybe, I was thinking, maybe I'm so programmed that I have to be in a learning situation. She read another page. "Just what in hell are you *doing?*" she burst out. I was frantic. "Just *read,*" I shouted. We got into a wild argument about the length of Gibbon's sentences.

Jill Sunderman took hold of my prick with a warm, soft, caressing towel.

My warm, soft prick.

She might have been tugging at the rope of a church bell. At the ear of a sleeping dog.

"Let's go out there by your bookcase," I whispered.

"Let's just get into bed," she whispered in reply.

"Just wait," I said.

"Please," she said. "Take the phone off the hook."

My God, another complication. Don't let them call us, she was saying. If Dorck wakes up, don't for a moment — Dorck was in his coma; somewhere in the course of the day it had dawned

58

on her that this time, now, she could do what she pleased. God-damn! She was whoopee *free*. From the boss hand. From the father-figuring eye. From the king's own brand of justice — The gate was sprung open. The fence was down. The tigers were loose. The cage was broken. The lonely falcon could seize the air.

And trust her luck, on this one damned night of her life when she had torn herself past the resisting bars, past the manacles, the chains, the slotted iron door: she lighted on me.

Professor, I had to do something. I felt guilty again. I felt guilty for what I wasn't doing. Your problem and mine, Proffo. Our predicament in a nutshell. How ironic: you do nothing, I do everything: we arrive at the same predicament. You dumb ass-hole.

I had no choice but to stall for time.

## 24

Jeremy, as usual, came up with one of his so-called ideas. "One thing before we hit the sack," he said. "I ought to run over to the university and take a look at the campus."

"Let's do it," you said. And even while you saved him from embarrassment, you gave him a twinge of dismay.

You got off the bus on the South Side; you walked westward along the bank of the North Saskatchewan River until you came to what must be a faculty club: through the picture windows you watched a crowd of people waving their arms and soundlessly shouting: they might have been drowning in a great beaker of tepid, stained water, trying each to save himself, each taking the other down: you were silent together in the healing snow, Jeremy and you. Safe in the safe snow.

After that you were simply lost for a while; willingly lost. You crossed a great field of trackless snow, held out your arms to the snowflakes. You lay down, Jill, your arms and legs flung out and moving; you were making a snow angel, you explained. And you lay still and the snow fell upon you.

"Get up," Jeremy insisted.

You stumbled onto a quiet sidewalk that ran in front of three buildings, three red brick and old and seedily elegant buildings that might have been dormitories but somehow were not. They gave you back a frightening silence. Two parkas seemed to be necking on a snow-covered bench; a girl looked out from a parka hood, into the falling snow, then gave back her mouth to her lover. You made paired footprints, Jeremy and you; there was no wind and the snowflakes heaped themselves into ghosts and owls on the branches of dark spruce.

A bearded man, lithe and quick-stepping, made taller by a fur cap, came out of a shadow and spoke to Jeremy: "Ross?" he said.

Jeremy said nothing.

"Excuse me," the stranger said. "I thought you were Ross."

You, very softly, let yourself laugh. At nothing.

Jeremy felt a chill as if he had heard a wolf out on the tundra. "I look like an arctic explorer," he explained. "Searching for the lost Franklin."

You were covered in snow, Jeremy and you. You were moving landscapes.

And then you came to the bright tall shadows of the Students' Union: you dusted each other free of snow.

Formless and silent, they sprawled, the students; their books open on their laps or on the floor, eyes shut. Somewhere, too far away to be heard clearly, a record was playing. The students, apparently, listened.

In the very mole bottom of that high building you found a group of young men, curling. You saw them through glass: they slid as they walked, as if they wore invisible skates or were only dreaming. They played without speaking, as if they were playing in their sleep, bending to set the bright rocks coasting up the ice, bending to sweep, then turning away indifferent before the last rock struck, into random disorder, the others. Out of the painted circles.

"Good heavenly Christ," Jeremy said. "Let's get the fuck out of here."

You did not know where you were going but found the bridge; entering onto the High Level Bridge, walking north, you could see far down the frozen river. Far down, to where a power station keeps the river open and the steam rises ghostly on the black water. But large and jagged flakes of snow tumbled on your heads; when you reached the middle of the bridge you were in a cloud of snow; only the rapping of the cars, their sounds echoing inside the bridge girders, gave assurance that you were not adrift in the sky.

In the middle of the bridge you caught his hand, stopped him; your faces came close together, held apart by the touch of snow.

"You don't have to," you said.

"Ha," he said. He pretended not to understand.

"You don't have to."

"I want to."

The snow moved between you, visible, as if generating its own light.

Jeremy's past overwhelmed him. In his own pause he heard Reggie say: "It's a form of recognition." Reggie eating chocolates, gulping them one, two. And Carol: "Just what in hell are you up to *now?*"

"I want to," he added. "I want to."

"I suppose it doesn't matter."

"Sure it matters," he said. "Of course it matters."

He went to the iron rail. He looked over the rail, down into the falling snow, trying to see the North Saskatchewan River. He let his mind dream the name. The name that had been so long in his dreaming. All those hours spent over a school atlas, studying maps. Finding blank spaces. Finding that thin blue line of river that melted out of the Rocky Mountains and fell across the northwest, into other thin blue lines, into Hudson Bay. Somewhere north of that river, Grey Owl lay cold in his grave.

Jeremy looked away from the rail. But he had to look again. At the sheer deep empty space that leapt up out of the tumbling snow.

"Nothing matters," you were saying.

And as you spoke you dared to trust your back to the little iron rail that fended off the emptiness.

In that moment, Jeremy was aroused. One is willing to grant him that unlikely supposition. But he insists that you, at the same moment, closed your eyes. Gave him your mouth. Let him tug at your coat, at your skirt, with his left hand, even while he fumbled with his right to find his zipper.

And there in that blear suspension in the sky, together you invited the whole blue city to express its amazement. Together you were caught on that rail, lurching and locked in a quick fury, lifted and hammered to the sky . . . while only inches beyond your aching and thrust bodies . . . beyond your hot joining, the empty and dread air held nothing for you but nothing. . . . The frosted hairs of your lost privacy might have curled and clamped, might have fused iron-hard, snared, strangled . . . and yet the angel was nowhere in the night. Only the horny heave, the deep rejoinder of gutteral delight —

It was sudden. It was all very sudden and short.

"Are you sorry?" he said.

Why did he ask such a painful question? Such a sad question.

In the strange light of night, in the snow, you were shaking your head.

## 25

By the way, Professor, I forgot to give you one little detail: I did leave the apartment briefly yesterday. I took a taxi downtown to the airlines office and I cashed in my return ticket. The truth is, I had to borrow money from Jill in order to get out of Notikeewin: and of course I want to repay her. What I have in mind is this: once the interview is over I'll simply phone Carol and tell her how it went. Then I'll have her ask you to wire me a bit of extra cash. Thus, by the time you hear this tape you will both have sent me the money and been repaid. A peculiar experience of time: to encounter, after the act, the thought that was father to the act.

This whole idea sets me to thinking about you. As I reconstruct the impulse now, it was at your suggestion that I applied for a job out here. I begin to suspect your motive. I know you have a professorial desire to exercise your impotence on my gullible wife, Professor Madham. Your lassitude appeals to her. Not to mention your huge head with its greying wavy hair, your squash-player's perfect figure, your Zapata mustache smelling, as Carol once idly remarked, of meerschaum pipes and rum and honey. I know you would add her upstate innocence to your collection of beautiful objects, use her to stimulate your failing appetites. And that is why you sent me out here into the eternal goddamned temptations of the wilderness. Into what you, in your appalling ignorance, like to *think* is the wilderness —

Which reminds me. What a hell of a night I had.

For some reason I got it into my head around midnight that with any luck at all I could crack off a dissertation by early dawn. I would announce to Chairman Balding, I just happen to have my dissertation with me. Finished it up with no sweat but haven't had a chance to proofread, hope you'll overlook a few typos. That's my wife's department.

Ha.

We shake hands.

He slaps me on the back.

I sat at the kitchen table in Jill Sunderman's apartment, the light coming over my left shoulder, the pencil held in the approved position. Jill's writing tablet under my pencil.

The time has come, I told myself: the beginning. Write a brief introduction. I wish to thank Professor R. Mark Madham for directing my attention . . . to my own continuing failure.

Wups. Tear out the page. Tear up the page. Walk over to the garbage container, step on the pedal, raise my right arm, pitch an inside curve drop.

I wish to thank the State University of New York at Binghamton for paying me an annual salary of two thousand dollars. Per annum. I wish to thank the Chairman, Department of English, State University of New York at Binghamton, for the use of a splintered desk on which I was permitted, yes, even encouraged, to grade one million themes and on which, without either permission or encouragement, I laid Miss Cohen. Also, as I recall, a Miss Petcock. Also, believe it or not, a Miss Kundt. And also, unless my memory fails me, an art major named Carol Scull. Who later became my wife.

I wish to thank my patient wife, presently of the Xerox Room, State University of New York at Binghamton, for accidentally using the thirty-eight pages of my fourth but not final dissertation in an attempt to start a fire, while sitting at Professor Madham's feet, in Professor Madham's imported Italian fireplace . . .

Wups. Tear out the page.

I struck on the marvellous notion that maybe a simple review of past dissertation attempts in lieu of the finished product might give to Chairman Balding some idea of the range and depth of my learning.

Good God, I thought to myself: I have neglected to thank Reggie.

To Reggie the Bull Dyke, a hearty thank you, for quickly finishing her own dissertation so that I might, in peace, get on with mine.

"Going Down With Orpheus."

Eighteen months and four hundred pages. Abandoned.

"The Artist as Clown and Pornographer."

Nine months of reading and three hundred index cards. Sold to an M.A. candidate for twenty dollars.

"The Columbus Quest: The Dream, the Journey, the Surprise."

Eighteen weeks. I couldn't get past the first sentence.

"Sadness," old Madham says to me one day, "there's only one problem in this world that you take seriously."

"Right," I said.

"No," he said. "I mean yes. Why did Archie Belaney become Grey Owl?"

"How," I said. I raised my right hand, the palm facing the good professor's beaming face. Why he was sweating I do not know.

"The story of a man," I agreed, "who died into a new life."

"He faked the death."

"But he woke up free nevertheless."

"Be serious."

"One false move, Professor, and instead of addressing you, I'll be you. That's serious."

Dawn came slowly to the eastern horizon. But still it came too fucking fast.

I awoke to find my head lying on the table like a gift on a platter, my neck very nearly broken. I tore up the writing tablet, lifted the lid of the garbage container, raised my right arm, pitched. A no-hitter.

I drew my trusty microphone.

"I'm hungry," Jill said.

"Can't you see I'm talking?"

"I'm hungry."

We were pretending that nothing had happened; she was pretending. I had work to do: the old secret, nail your resolve to the desk. Glue your ass to the chair. Pick up the pencil.

I insisted that I take her out to an expensive breakfast in an expensive restaurant, to celebrate the forthcoming interview. An occasion not to be neglected, never to be forgotten.

But as we were crossing the High Level Bridge, almost at the spot where we had paused the previous evening, we found ourselves being delayed by an old pick-up truck: a dog sleigh was lashed securely to the top of the cab: a number of dogs watched sleepily from inside the open flaps on the back of the truckbox.

"Follow that vehicle," I said to Jill.

She didn't hear me. A train on the deck above us, going the other way, made it impossible for her to hear.

"FOLLOW THAT INDIAN," I shouted. In the sudden silence.

"You're crazy," Jill said.

"That truck," I explained.

An Indian was at the wheel. I'd seen that when he glanced back to check on his dogs. A woman and a number of children were seated to his right.

We followed our Pied Piper out of the City of Edmonton, past the turn-off to the International Airport, past every cafe and diner and greasy spoon that came into sight. By 9:30 a.m. on the dot we were walking into the decorated basement of the First Presbyterian Church.

The church ladies were serving a pancake breakfast on the first morning of the first day of the 27th Annual Notikeewin Winter Festival. How the Indian knew exactly where to find those pancakes is a mystery to me. He started out with a double order. I handed my tape recorder to Jill and told her to find us a place to sit.

A lady was putting six pancakes onto my paper plate.

"How do you do, Judge?" she said.

All the ladies around her burst into laughter.

I was flabbergasted. Again. As usual. I turned away without butter. And there on the wall was a poster proclaiming that a certain Jeremy Sadness of New York, would, on this same night — TODAY TODAY TODAY — select the festival's reigning queen.

"This is deceit," I said. "This is a moral outrage. Who the hell is this Jeremy Sadness? Who is this imposter on the poster? Ha."

Jill was nowhere to be seen.

I was alone. I was absolutely starving.

The tables were crowded; I sat down with the Indian and his wife and their four small sons. Something like eight willing hands passed me the syrup. But no one would speak. There I sat in my buckskin jacket and my braids and my moccasins, and I might as well have been invisible.

Jill came up behind me and touched a finger to my neck. I damned near jumped off the bench.

"I have to leave you," she whispered.

"WHY?" I demanded. The joint was crowded with a lot of people who were determined to get started on a three-day spree. They were talking too loud. They were forcing their laughter. "Eat your breakfast."

"I've no time. The queen has to be selected here tonight — and the stage isn't ready. And I've other things to do." She joined in the laughter. "Good luck."

I turned around to catch at her wrist.

"Dorck," I called. "Isn't he up? Isn't he out of the sack and back on the job?"

She was almost at the door. "Be here at midnight. To judge."

Then I noticed she still had my tape recorder. Maybe she'd

taken it by accident: but without it I'd be lost. "Wait," I shouted. "Stay."

I was left with all those slicked-up stoic Indians. Two of the little boys were giggling together. Their mother said something in their native tongue and they began to eat.

"What do you think about this?" I demanded of the Indian beside me. "What choice has a man got in this world?"

"You are going to judge?" he inquired.

"Yes," I said.

"Judge what?"

"The women. The most beautiful woman."

"I see," he said.

He buried his big wide face in his pancakes. His goddamned big Cree face; I knew he was Cree by the way he kept quiet.

I did a few quick grip exercises.

"Is there some reason why I shouldn't judge?" I wanted to know. "I think I know something about women. I've done some graduate work in that area of specialization. I'll tell you one damned thing —"

His ears turned to stone. He was a lean, wiry fellow with a brush-cut; his left hand was badly scarred. He couldn't hear me. He filled his mouth with butter and syrup and a pancake and he couldn't speak.

"Did you ever hear of Grey Owl?" I shouted at him.

You couldn't change your mind in that place, it was so full of customers. I resented their presence. I was a native and they were intruding: city slickers in red woollen coats, businessmen in coonskin, women in Gay Nineties bustles. Skiers who wouldn't part with their skis. Little girls in short skirts, carrying their figure skates. A gang of boys brandishing hockey sticks.

I felt a little bit threatened, I guess. Insecure. I was thinking of Professor Balding's secretary, watching down the hall for the new man. He didn't hear me. That Indian didn't hear me.

"Grey Owl!" I repeated. "Did you ever run into Grey Owl?"

The Indian looked up from his plate, looked across the table at his wife. "Grey Owl?" he said.

His wife giggled.

One of the little boys saw his chance. "Why is his hair that way?" he asked his mother.

"Tell those kids to eat their pancakes," the Indian said. "I'll be late for the race."

"Why —" the little boy insisted.

Wham. Right across the knuckles with a syrupy fork.

I got up. It was too much. I drank my coffee standing up, I burned the roof of my mouth. I left.


## 26

I was arrested right outside the church basement door.

Two redcoats seized me by the wrists as I stepped into the winter day.

"Here he is," one of them said.

"He did it," the other one said.

"Did what?" I said. My eyes weren't used to the blinding, blurred light. "I'm innocent."

They slapped a pair of handcuffs on me.

"Resisted arrest," the first redcoat said. "Make a note of it, corporal."

Applause. The people in the line-up waiting to get at the pancakes gave the redcoats a round of applause. Justice, once again, was being served.

It was a game I guess. I tried to rub at my eyes — there was a kind of ice fog in the air — but I found myself handcuffed.

The corporal saw my confusion. "It's for a worthy cause," he whispered. Then he raised his voice: "Come along, sir. To the crowbar hotel."

The Chamber of Commerce buccaneers who own the town are dressed up in the uniforms of the North West Mounted Police. They've built a fake jailhouse of spruce slabs on a hayrack — on a sleigh being pulled by a fine team of blue roan mares. I found myself climbing and stumbling into the hoosegow: the inmates began to gibe and holler as the lock clanked shut behind me.

"I want to see my lawyer."

"Get this rapist out of our cell."

"Somebody bribe the warden."

The team jogged along, the runners of the sleigh riding lightly on the packed snow. Now and then we stopped, at a service station or a bank or a restaurant, and the police singled out another victim for arrest. Purely at random. They picked up the driver of a car for wearing glasses. They clapped irons on a pedestrian for waiting for a light to turn green. They arrested two dogs for conduct unbecoming a lady.

We were carried through the streets. The crowds on the sidewalks shouted and waved: little boys ran out and hung on behind the sleigh and slid on their overshoes on the snow and fell down, and still they hung on.

We prisoners amused ourselves by looking through the cracks between the spruce slabs. At the poor devils out there in the naked light, wandering aimless and ignored. We were special. We were the chosen. We had the bond of our bondage.

I saw a real policeman and I shouted, "Arrest that man. For carrying a concealed weapon."

Pretty girls came out of stores and shops to throw kisses at our unknown fate. Now it was our turn to shout and wave. We coasted through the decorated streets, under the flap of the welcoming flags.

Everywhere the redcoats found more victims. We resented the newcomers, we old trusties; the jail was ours. We were there first. "Booo," we said to a man arrested for coming out of a doorway. "Shame," we cried, at a man picked up for not throwing snowballs.

Then the jail was jammed full and we were only on display: we were carried past Our Lady of Sorrows Hospital. To give cheer to the inmates, I suppose. They waved from the windows. They came out of doors on crutches and in wheelchairs, recklessly abandoning all rules and regulations in order to see us, to nod and smile in the snow.

"Dorck," I shouted. Up at a closed window in the hospital. "Get us out of here, Dorck. Bail us out of this mess. Pull a few strings."

We went down to the end of that street to turn around: in front of the Notikeewin Memorial Gardens.

The street was suddenly empty. We could see out to an empty field. But an old man was in the graveyard, shovelling snow. Digging in the snow.

"Arrest that man," somebody shouted. "For digging a hole."
We all chuckled a little.

"Arrest that man for disregarding the public welfare."

"Arrest that man for indecent exposure."

It was cold in that damned cage. Some of the victims had been snatched away from offices and doorways, and didn't have adequate clothing. I volunteered to keep a young secretary warm; she took me up on it. I opened my buckskin jacket and she snuggled inside, against me. Her back to me and my arms up high around her waist.

You guessed it. Up came old Diogenes. The Cynic. An iron will after all. I'd had a bad moment with Jill, I can tell you that; there in her apartment when she was ready for bed. I explained about the forthcoming interview, my temporary anxiety, the need to polish up my dissertation. She fell asleep, I guess — But that secretary: she was in a festive frame of mind. She was shorter than Jill. Or Miss Cohen. Or, as I recall, Miss Kundt. But her ass was bedrock firm and warmer than new-baked bread. Long as the ride was, it was hardly long enough. I was sorry to see our destination.

We pulled out onto the ice of Elkhart Pond.

A huge and raucous crowd had gathered around the ice fort.

The fort itself — Fort Duhamel, they call it — is made entirely of ice. Great blocks of ice that glitter a pale green-white have been mortared with freezing water and stacked into two high walls. Two loop-holed and serrated walls. In the shielded angle made by the joined walls is what appears from the outside to be a blockhouse, under the Red Maple Leaf: in fact it is a stepped dais. Of ice that is carved and colored.

In the center of the dais is a huge ice chair.

To the left of that chair — that throne — sat one man, holding a sheaf of papers and a microphone. To the right three smiling girls were sitting in a row on a bench of ice.

On the throne itself there slumped a drowsing white bear.

The team of horses pulled the sleigh into the fort. And stopped. At that moment the bear stirred. The sleeping bear stirred, stretched, began to wake up, yawned its mouth hugely open.

The crowd burst into a deafening roar that chilled the very marrow of my bones. Mother of God.

Only then did I realize our arrival had signalled the official opening of the 27th Annual Notikeewin Winter Festival.

The bear straightened and sat looking comically human on the throne.

The mayor of Notikeewin stood up. I guess he made a speech.

I was holding on for dear life to that festive secretary and staring in disbelief at the three beautiful maidens who were cooling their bottoms on that bench of solid ice. This is criminal, I thought.

I'm damned: that old bear never once looked away from where I was peeking through a crack.

"It must be a real bear," I whispered to the secretary.

"Ordinarily," the secretary whispered in reply, "Mr. Dorck is the bear."

"This year," I said, "he's hibernating. Ha."

"He judges," the secretary continued. She moved my left hand higher on a full breast. "The bear judges. We'll each of us have to face the bear."

A dozen redcoats sprang into action. They opened the jail-house door and took out a prisoner and led him up onto the dais.

"Charge?" the bear said.

"Pride, lust and sloth."

The mayor was holding the microphone for the bear.

"Charge dismissed," the bear said. "He's only a man."

Then I knew: it was the voice of Bea Sunderman. It was the unmistakable voice —

The crowd was applauding.

Now the victims were being arranged in a neat line by the redcoats.

"Charge?" the bear said. To the next victim.

The corporal read from an imaginary book. "Walking on two legs."

"Fine: two dollars," the bear said.

The prisoner dug into his pockets to find his wallet.

"Charge?" the bear was saying to the next prisoner.

All charges, I recognized, had changed since the time of arrest. I would not then, it appeared, be charged with resisting arrest.

"Charge?" the bear was saying.

"Cowardice, desertion, flight."

"Charge dismissed," the bear said. "He's only a man."

And then I knew something else. Bea Sunderman had recognized her chance. Dorck was out cold, dead asleep. He was out of the game. And she was able to exercise the gavel, the hammer, of justice. Bea Sunderman had seized the scales and the sword.

The secretary was summoned away from my hot and desperate embrace. With a little wiggle of her behind she saluted and was gone.

I soon would be summoned also.

I must go before Bea Sunderman to be judged. My hard-on would not go down. A kind of terror came over my eyes. Nothing was changing; it should have been changing. The ebb, after the flow. The moon in the male. Maybe, I thought wildly, I can whack myself off in the next thirty seconds. Last one to finish is a rotten egg. No. I would appear before the mirrors of justice with a bone-on that wouldn't quit. Criminal, see thyself. Charge: erection without end. Fine: flogging is not good enough. For such scoundrels.

I tried to think it through. Relax, I told myself.

The secretary was facing her charge.

"Falsifying the evidence," the corporal reported.

"Nonsense," I burst out. A lie, I thought to myself. A downright lie. What has happened to truth?

The secretary giggled. "Innocent," she cried.

"Endure your innocence," the bear said. "Go free."

Satyriasis, I told myself. This bone-on will never go away. Will never slip into obscurity. Not a chance in the wide world. I must go through life with this thing waving in front of me like the loading boom on a freighter. Pointing at the stars. I'm cursed. These damned women have cursed me, have cast a spell on my prick. Now they've really done me in. I'm destined to lug this trunk of a dead tree, this bogus column of marble from nation to nation, from epoch to epoch. . . . Miss Cohen, you were absolutely right. Talk about a tragic goddamned passion. Reggie, you did this to me: you and your goddamned Pandora's box of cheap chocolates. Charge: hubris. Fine: eternity of same. If only Carol could judge this one. Inadequate, she would say. No refinement. Too physical. Penalty: a crown of fire.

"Sir," a redcoat was saying. "Step out here please."

I was almost the last person in the prison. I was the last person.

I flung myself down flat on my back. It looked as if I was resisting arrest. Dissertation Number Six, I thought: Christopher Columbus, not knowing that he had not come. . . . A beautiful sentence. A finely wrought sentence; honed. If only —

"Sir," the redcoat said. "You'll have to cooperate. We want to get this over with."

It worked. I lay down, it lay down. Thank God. Like that, it was gone, vanished. Flop. Kerplunk. Another victory for the ice. Thank God for the old certainties.

I leaped to my feet. To the door.

"Hurray!" I said to the waiting crowd.

It was then I noticed the magpie carved in the ice of the bear's throne. An elegant bird, the magpie, for all its reputation.

"Charge?" The bear looked closely at me. "Who is this mortal man?"

"He's a judge, Your Honor."

The crowd was amused.

"What does this man judge?"

"He judges beauty, Your Honor."

The three girls sitting to the right of the throne were rosy now with blush and anticipation. And only at that fraught moment did I realize: one of them would occupy the throne, would reign throughout the festival.

And I, come blackest midnight, would choose.

They looked exactly alike. All three of them. On that bench of solid and snatch-chilling ice.

"How did you get the job?" the bear asked.

That was too much. That did it right there and then. I was at that very instant no doubt scheduled to be chatting with a chairman or a dean about my dissertation. My thesis is simply this, sir: Man, in seeking out the unknown, came only to the discovery that his feet are being sucked into the quicksand and quagmire of stinking death; while he lingers on in life his balls and his brain are caught in the virulence and vise of his fatal impulse to seek out the unknown.

"I was given no choice," I said.

The crowd booed.

"Then tell us," the bear said, "is it better to be beautiful or to be happy?"

She riddled me a tough one. I was close to a cold sweat, wishing I could get hold of that microphone. Ask Jill, I thought to myself: ask your daughter. She drove over icy roads and knocked on the door of her own apartment, a terrified stranger.

I said nothing.

"Fine," the bear said. "Exactly."

The crowd laughed.

"Then tell us further," the bear said, "is it better to seek beauty or to seek truth?"

Again I had nothing to say. You should meet our poor dear Madham, I thought. He would stumble between a woman's legs while staring into her eyes. The crowd surged into a closing circle, threatened me with a chorus of boos. I was ready and willing to run for it. Make a break. But where would I go?

"Exactly," the bear said. "And now, Mr. Judge, please, tell us one last thing."

Last thing all right. And last things. My specialty since the beginning. Bringing up the rear.

I nodded.

She either nodded in reply, or bent her head and licked at her fur.

"Tell these three waiting princesses. Is it better to be beautiful, or is it better to be free?"

Excellent question, I decided. Excellent. Consult Mr. Dorck for details. He kicked himself loose from gravity itself.

Those three girls — those three abashed and sighing maidens up there watching me, slowly turning into blocks of ice — they were trying to detect the slightest whim or preference. Trying to read the future in my silence.

They looked exactly alike. They had on fur coats. I could hardly see them. They were the spitten image of each other, I could see that much. And I was elected to be judge. Given the microphone, I could have made a speech. I turned away.

And then I noticed something else. I saw that Indian. With his wife and his sons and one of his dogs. Everyone else in the crowd was laughing. But that damned Cree Indian with his brush-cut wasn't. He was watching me as if my life was at stake. That's when I answered.

"I love you," I said. To the bear. "You are happy and wise and free."

The bear fell silent for more than a moment. Dead silent. I thought I had her. Then she said loudly into the microphone: "This man is charged with loving a bear."

"Hang him," someone in the crowd shouted. "Hang him. Hang him," they shouted. "Get a rope. String him up."

We were standing very close to the spot where young Robert Sunderman plunged through the ice. While chasing a puck that he himself had shot out onto the pond. I guess, if anything, I envied him. I thought the ice might open. Then close again. The ice healing. The healing ice. And I didn't believe for a moment that he had troubled to come back after.

Bear-lover. Hanged.

The bear raised her right paw. The crowd fell silent.

I noticed the Indian again. He was only watching. Waiting.

"The charge," the bear repeated, "loving a bear." She had made up the charge herself; the corporal hadn't had a chance to exercise his callous wit.

"Charge dismissed," the bear said. "Go free yourself."

She pointed.

We all turned away from the throne to look across the pond.

The figure of a man tipped over the edge, onto the slope of the tall wooden ski jump, began to move, began to slip, caught his balance, raised his arms, swept on down the graded slope, took off into the air, soared up at the blinding sun: and then was motionless, flying.

## 27

How do you woo a bear?

I went looking for my Indian friend, to get some honest advice. I found him at the starting post. At his starting post.

A dozen short posts or stakes were fixed in the ice in a row across the Cree River. To each was tied the rear of a dogsled; and something like eight or nine sleigh dogs were trying to tear each sled free and away. The tangle of dogs and harness and sleighs was nothing short of chaotic; the yapping and howling were only deafening. And that wasn't enough for what I needed.

A policeman kept the crowd back. I was trying to circle around him, to seek out and approach my friend in the confusion of officials and mushers and helpers, when the starting shot was fired.

Each musher flung off the rope that anchored his team to a post.

And then the chaos unravelled into a dozen streaking dog teams, the mushers yelling, swinging their whips, running beside their lead dogs, riding the runners of their sleighs and calling, "Gee." "Ha."

They were headed upriver, going away. Friend, I wanted to shout against all that din, wait. I have something to ask you. Listen. About bears. Are they too concerned with the rendering of happiness, the prevention of pain?

But already the mushers' backs were growing smaller, bent forward over the disappearing sleighs. Now and then a whip rose up, but made no noise that we could hear. The teams were spreading out, finding their pace, their strategies.

They had fifty miles to go, running upriver and then doubling back. I asked the policeman how long they'd be gone.

"It's pretty fair trail weather," he told me. "Be here in three hours if you want to see the winner come in."

I had three hours to kill. I went back to Elkhart Pond.

The festival is in full swing. I want to tell you, everything has become a game in this mad place: wood-splitting, ice-cutting, flour-packing, log-sawing. Moose-callers are calling moose: I expect a great awkward animal to lumber out of a coulee and onto Elkhart Pond, quietly munching the hats off people's heads. Goose-callers call geese: whole honking flights of Canada geese should come down out of the sky and skid to a halt on the unexpected ice.

New competitions are announced on the hour: men who have worn themselves out at one task rush to wear themselves out at another. Great hordes of admirers hurry from one place to another, breathless to see another competition.

Combat, goddamnit, that's what it is. Trial by strength. Trial by chance. Trial by wager. Trial by drowning in your own sweat.

Trial by freezing your balls off. Trial by falling. Trial by flying.

It was the ski jumpers who held me most: those mortal men lifting off, soaring motionless in the cold air: and of a sudden, landing, sweeping downhill to a halt.

I had watched maybe ten jumpers, when a strange-looking figure caught my eye. A skier in a cowboy hat.

He looked familiar. I watched as he adjusted his bindings, up there on the scaffold, pulled on his woollen mittens. Pulled on his desperate passion to fly.

He crouched, tipped forward and down; he came off the end of the in-run; he leaped forward, out.

"Yeeeeaaaahooo," he shouted.

We loved that crazy cowboy, mounting that invisible horse.

And then he was up in the air, leaning forward, stiffly forward, so that his cowboy hat was over the tips of his skis. His arms were rigid at his sides. He kept on going up, up, then forward, then forward. The watching crowd gave out a gasp of wonder: that wild cowboy was riding nothing but the cold air. The arc of his rising, it seemed, would never break.

And then he landed. He took the shock awkwardly; his knees didn't give in quite the right way. I thought he would fall. But he stayed on his skis, he swerved, skidded into a round of applause.

I saw him more closely now. He was the man who had given me a lift from the Airport to Notikeewin.

For awhile I was content to watch: the jumpers' control and form, the courage that fused those virtues into grace. I watched the judges and wondered how they might choose, and maybe that's why I had to talk to the bronc buster. I sought him out and found him at the base of the scaffold, waiting to jump again. Like some damned fool rooster that only recently had learned his ancestors were creatures of the air.

He recognized me right away. "Hey," he said. "Good to

see you. You down here for the trap-setting contest?"

"What the hell are you doing," I encountered, "trying to capture a cloud?"

There wasn't a trace of a cloud in the sky.

"Nothing to it," the cowboy said. "You live on these flatlands long enough, you get mad one day and build yourself a hill." He tapped the base of the scaffold.

"But why jump off it?" I said.

"You win this purse, you got something."

"A broken leg," I said. "The way you land on those skis."

"You go up — you're bound to come down. It's that easy."

It was the cowboy's turn, and he climbed the log and timber scaffold. As if he might be settling onto a bronco in a chute, waiting for the gate to open. I walked down the slope to watch him land. God knows, I went to a ski resort one time, hoping to get laid, and I went around on crutches for nine weeks.

I wasn't halfway down the slope when the air was split by a mighty "Yeeeeaaaahoooo."

And then, before I could get in position to watch him land, I heard a great gasp come out of the crowd's throat.

I looked up into the sun.

That cowboy was up there all right, in the sky. Flying. But his skis were crossed. He was a windmill up there. A turning wheel. A drowning swimmer who could find no water that might save him. He wasn't leaning out and forward, stiff, controlled. The grace was gone out of him. He was snapped together, curled up, his knees choked under his face, his awkward feet turned into sails. Some terrible joker had turned his spurs into skis. In the draw he had pulled a sunfishing bronco.

And then he wasn't riding at all. He was plummeting. He ripped off his hat with his mittened right hand and gave it a reckless flourish.

81

I couldn't get through the crowd.

"Looked like he was riding old Midnight," I heard someone say.

"Give him air," someone was saying close to the bottom of the slope. "Give him air. He can't breathe."

And then I heard the first wail of the siren. The ambulance got to my cowboy friend before I could see him off.

I was left alone again.

## 28

He landed on his head.

One rumor has it that he's dead, the cowboy is dead: the hospital won't let word out, for fear it will spoil the festival. But another rumor says he's silly in the rafters: he sits in his hospital room saying over and over, "I see with a new clarity."

They won't let visitors in to visit.

"What do you see?" a nurse asks him.

"Now I see," he replies. "Now I see the snow. Now I see the sun. The sky, incidentally, is very close to the earth."

Another rumor has it that he's not in his hospital room at all: the officials paid him good money to go back home and stay the hell out of the games.

I walked down Elkhart Creek to where it joins the Cree River. It was quiet down there on the river. I had to think. Learning to fall, I was thinking: that's the trick. Flying is easy. The whole, the absolute mastery resides in knowing how to fall. And by Jesus, I'm a living specialist.

We were a handful of marooned survivors, staring up the river at absolutely nothing. The valley was drifted an impossible white in the afternoon glare of sun; the hills made no shadows; the clumps of poplar and spruce were landmarks without design. Only the river itself offered a way: you must follow its surface with your feet, almost with the tips of your fingers, in order to see.

People with cameras gathered together around me. They would capture and save whatever the victory that emerged from that silence. We waited. One fencepost, up the valley, apparently without a fence, tried in that quivering light to become a dog. A man. A bear. Then we were a crowd, staring upriver to where the earth and the sky made one bright haze.

And then, out of our dream perhaps, out of our own waiting, out of the very sky itself and around the farthest bend of the river, came two sleighs.

They disappeared. Into a hollow, perhaps. Taking a shortcut. Or maybe it was our confidence that lost them.

They invented a horizon. They would not come to us at all, but would draw a circle on our vanishing.

It was a long time before I realized they had run closer. The moving dogs were given legs.

The dogs were trotting, nine dogs in each team, strung out neatly, noses down to the frozen trail. They seemed hardly to be in a hurry. It was that that affected me most, at the very goal itself: the quiet precision of the dogs, their enduring patience. Their quick paws.

One of the teams was that of the Cree. He was running now, to keep the sleigh light. Now and then he swung his whip: only as a gesture to make himself keep up. We were all so quiet we could hear those two men, speaking to their dogs.

But what could they say to those dogs, then? People are waiting to cry us home? Friends are waiting? We heard the flow of their ancient syllables: the two men speaking commands that were little prayers. The curses that were affection. I needed my tape recorder: given a microphone I could have spoken, might have made a speech on silence and children and heroic dogs and victorious men; on the eloquence of watching; on the mother lighting the lamp in the frosted window, the wife or mistress hearing the lost voice break the stillness of the night, cracking the black air. . . . But the two men only uttered sounds: out of hoarse throats, the driven breath. At the very finish line itself.

It was the ending of the race that did me in. The two teams were running side by side, the mushers side by side. They might have been chatting. They might have been uneasy, staying together, facing the waiting strangers.

And then, hardly beyond the victory, the Cree stepped onto his sleigh. And I swear to this, I could see from where I was waiting: he touched the brake that is under the sleigh. The forked, crabbed branch of a tree. The antler of wood turned anchor. "Chu," he was telling his dogs. In Cree. Turn left. Cross the line.

But he was touching the sleigh's brake.

We cheered the winning musher in. Joe — his name from the loudspeaker lost in applause — Prince Albert, Saskatchewan. Home of Champions. . . . Yes, I thought, I know: Grey Owl, dying in a Prince Albert hospital, congestion in his lungs. I can't breathe. The old nuns praying for his soul. I can't breathe, I can't breathe. The hunter who would not, finally, hunt. The killer refusing to kill. Saving the beaver. The wracked body of the truest Indian of them all, that strayed Englishman — that corpse carried north again, the team of horses, the sleigh, moving in solemn procession across the ice of the lake, into the bush. Into the wilderness. The shod hoofs of the horses, iron on the spring ice. The eight quick legs of the horses. Moving to the end.

The lead dog crossed the line. The two dogteams crossed the finish line almost side by side. But the difference of six feet, after those fifty miles, made one man a loser.

"Three hours. Forty minutes. Nine seconds."

A car with a loudspeaker mounted on top was parked at the finish line; a man with a microphone in one hand, a stop watch in the other, was greeting the winner.

"Joe," he was asking, "how do you feel after winning?"

"Dead."

Joe was panting hard, mopping the sweat off his face with a woollen shirt he picked up out of a canvas bag on the sleigh.

"Joe, what's the secret of your winning?"

"My wife." Joe was trying hard to catch his breath. "She makes good dog feed."

He had won before, he had answered all these questions before. He was impatient, ready with the answers before the questions came. He tried to smile for the cameras.

"Joe, what are you going to do with all the prize money?"

"Spend it."

The crowd laughed its appreciation.

I walked over to where a few people were standing in a ragged circle around the Cree Indian and his sleigh and his dogs. He was sweating too; his wife handed him a coke and he drank it thirstily, standing still behind his sleigh. His wife was there. She was, I could see, very proud of him. His four little sons were picking ice out of the paws of two of the dogs.

He had thrown the race, that Indian. I was certain: a few yards from victory he had touched his moccasin to the hooked branch of a tree that functioned as a brake. As an anchor. The dogs did not know why they were delayed.

The dogs took my attention. They had fallen flat on the packed snow, panting, the frosted fur moving beautifully over their lungs and their ribs. They gnawed at the snow, managed to get enough snow into their mouths to slake their thirst.

Their magnificent indifference held me. Filled me with admiration. Appalled me.

Appalled me, yes. Neither victory nor defeat mattered. Not at all. To them. I watched those beautiful dogs.

The Cree saw me watching; he looked at me for recognition. He had thrown the race. I couldn't meet his gaze. I couldn't give him that.

I couldn't ask about loving a bear.

The man on the loudspeaker was announcing the commencement of the 12-mile snowshoe race. He was telling the competitors to go get ready out on the snow on the river.

It was the dogs, not the Indian, that made me decide to run. I'll show that fucking dumb redskin, I said to myself, how to win.

## 29

I had never worn snowshoes in my life. On those occasions when we needed them on Sullivan Street, they weren't available. But I remembered the drawings in one of Grey Owl's books, the pencilled notation: "snowshoe lifts in front only, hanging by toe bridle."

There were extra snowshoes on hand, provided by a sporting goods store to interest potential customers in a new dimension of winter pleasure. I borrowed a pair of Athapaskan round-toed snowshoes. I watched as the other racers put theirs on; I secured mine, fastened mine, to my moccasined feet. It was as if I had, in anticipation of having to run, anchored myself to the very earth itself. This fits the pattern, Sadness, I told myself: now wait until they freeze to the ice. I tried to walk a few awkward steps. I caught the toe of the snowshoe under a crust of snow and fell. I was helped back onto my feet. "Don't walk," my guide and counsellor said. "This is something else."

I tried running. Loping. That was easier. A kind of unexpected rhythm came into my loins. Running suits me, I thought.

I discovered the necessary motion, the knees not working close together but slightly apart, the pace extended. I felt like a bear that was learning to dance.

We were told where we'd have to run. Six miles down the river valley. To the base of a huge trestle bridge. Don't, we were warned, go out on the ice beneath the bridge: it is always thin. Stop at the river's edge. Then six miles back.

It sounded simple.

We formed a ragged line, out across the river ice beside the stakes that had held the dogteams in check. There might have been thirty of us forming the line. I was trying to count when the starting gun sounded.

Just that fast, I was bringing up the rear.

Ha, I told myself, this is the strategy: I watched the other racers, saw that the trick was to set a pace I could maintain, loping at last into a dramatic victory. My shoulders began to loosen up; I was breathing deeply for the first time in something like nine years. I remembered my grip developers and opened and closed my hands with a new confidence. It had always been my intention, once my grip was developed, to move on to the rehabilitation of the next set of failing muscles. "Let me choose," my wife insisted.

I had feet. I had real feet. I looked down and counted them, one two one two, I watched the insidious method of their stealth. The straps of the snowshoes cut into them in a comforting fashion: each step was an achieved fraction of the way forward. An accomplishment.

I was totally alone: what surprised me was not the aloneness itself, but the silence that accompanied it. I felt some need to fill it up: yes, I explained to myself, identify the precision of your body, Sadness. Rejoice in it, an end in itself. And note: beyond morality, beyond the things of the mind, beyond choice itself: the will of the body to go on. Very profound, Sadness. Deep. Heavy. I was making good time. I was pleased with myself and therefore let Jill slip her way into my recollections. Memory alone, I explained, converts the ravening of lust into the mystery of love. But Carol spoke into my memory: Yes, Jeremy. You did well. You came well. You shuddered. A little on the quick side, yes, but at least you shuddered. Congratulations. The primitive self reasserting itself. And that one, low pre-literate outcry was surely interesting. Now bye-dee-bye and sleep tight —

A flock of chickadees got out of my path, chattered up from a bush of frozen berries. They were a sure sign: a storm was heading our way. I thought of myself plunging on through a blizzard, finding those who had collapsed in their panicky haste on the trail, giving them hope, getting them together in a makeshift igloo, then daring myself into the unknown to find our lost rescuers.

I passed a runner. Or rather, met one. He had turned around and was coming back. "Fuck it," he said to me.

I felt better. Now I was no longer the last man. I managed to speed up a little. The muscles in my calves were working like rawhide thongs; the snowshoes lifted me over the whispering snow. What should I think about? I asked myself.

My mind was as clear as the sky itself. I was seeing better, I recognized that: I was a free man, loping like a coyote down the river valley. The air was just cold enough to strike a balance against my new sense of warmth and energy. I was in my prime, by God. I could feel my belly muscles tightening up, lifting the slap and romp of my pecker into a new authority.

Then I actually passed a runner. Granted, he had simply quit. He was sitting in the snow trying to remove his snowshoes. He had got one off and it was sticking up in the snow, but the harness of the second was knotted, apparently. I waved as I went by, hardly breaking my stride.

The valley was full of silence: the south slope of the river hills was forested now, in green spruce and the hard limbs of poplar and berry bush. The north slope, facing into the sun, showed even through snow the red and grey of eroded coulees, the baked clay ribs of its summer.

I saw a rabbit. The rabbit was sitting perfectly still, white in the white snow of the valley floor. I noticed the black tips of its ears. I swerved to scare up the rabbit and it leaped lightly over the snow; I followed. Only to lose it when it stopped: froze.

Apparently, while trying to spot the vanished rabbit, I outdistanced some of the runners who were running. I was surprised to have passed them. Then I was surprised to look back and see how tired they looked. I was, I understood, getting my second wind. Heir to that mystery, I took longer strides, began to move with some secret deliberation.

The snow was a garden. Flowers of light and shadow bloomed out of the banks of the frozen river, out of the mouth of a cave, the curve of what must be stone, under the blue snow. A broken crow's nest in a crooked poplar had sprouted petals of light. A fallen tree had raised up the blown snow into a mound beneath its fall, and the mound splintered the fall of the sun's rays. A patch of fractured and reset ice was an alpine meadow of varied white, and where a spring had cracked loose from the winter itself the bent grasses were fixed in blossoms of translucent glass.

I was beginning to sweat. I could smell my own intent. I had on too many clothes; my buckskin jacket by itself weighed a stinking ton and was holding me back.

I dodged around a crater in the snow; a dip, I decided, that must conceal a buffalo wallow. A lone tree in the distance was a rubbing tree. I decided that too. Buffalo trails, deep ruts in the hidden earth, came down through the coulees, down to the slow river and the salt licks and the water. I swear I could smell the blood of a buffalo jump: right there in those hills the Cree and the Blackfoot drove the unknown herds to a fatal leap. Over the cliffs the buffalo lunged to the heaped bones below.

I stumbled.

There was nothing under my feet that might have tripped me. I caught my balance immediately.

I had arrived, without expecting it, at the turning point. Just like that: I caught myself before I stepped onto the ice of the river. I could hear running water, of a sudden: I looked up, straight ahead, and I saw the black threads of water themselves seemingly caught in grotesquely broken and sculptured chunks and slabs of ice: great blocks of ice that had been caught by the timbers that were the pillars of the bridge. I looked up: and above me the crossed and braced and stacked timbers rose, tier upon tier, to the colorless sky. I turned.

Only in turning did I discover that a dozen and more contestants were now behind me, not ahead.

I became prey to the fatal notion that I might win. As I did when I invited a certain Miss Scull briefly to seek employment in the Xerox Room while I completed all requirements for the ultimate graduate degree. As I did one time in a beer-drinking contest after I had chugalugged only four bottles of Schlitz. When I might have paced myself merely to survive, I spurred myself into a quicker motion.

I got my third wind. It was not quite so strong as my second wind. I got my fourth wind.

The muscles inside my thighs were beginning to ache. I entertained the notion that, in flinging each leg outward and forward, I might perchance fling one of them off, thus leaving myself awkwardly stranded in the midst of a pending blizzard on one leg. Even while quickening my pace, I checked with both hands my strained balls.

The snowshoes carried me over the snow, yet at each step I felt that I was sinking: the sheer weight of me turned each foot into a suction cup. That's when I took off my jacket. Running all the while, I pulled it off, somehow persuaded that draped over my arm it might be less encumbering.

The sweat on my back, in my hairy armpits, was effectively chilled: having achieved the appropriate temperature, it turned into ice. I wrenched myself free from that sudden cocoon.

Stimulated and refreshed, I told myself to run. Run, I thought. But against that thought I thought: on the seventh dissertation, he rested. "Collapse: The Theory and the Practice."

It was then I threw away my buckskin jacket. I dropped it in the middle of a wide field of snow where I might easily spot it later. I promised myself that I would borrow another pair of snowshoes and gallop another circuit in order, later, to retrieve it from the snow.

Stripped of the heavy jacket I was striding forward with a new ease. I passed a runner who had fallen from exhaustion, who was on his hands and knees, trying to get to his feet. I believe he was vomiting in the snow.

We were running upriver now. We were running west, into the sun. I discovered that the slight blur before my eyes was in fact my eyelashes, swinging like windshield wipers. I ran with my head flung back. I believe it was Miss Kundt who claimed she was seduced by my eyelashes: they intruded now on the magnificent vision of space that assailed me.

I thought of Miss Kundt, and I could not imagine her standing up. She lived at the south end of one of Binghamton's closed and collapsed bridges; sometimes, lost and stymied, I strayed my way to her door and found her lying naked on her carpeted floor, reading a book. Miss Kundt was always naked. Always reading a book. She wanted to go into city-planning: she had a theory about randomness, the importance of the sudden, the unexpected, in our experience of the city block. She was writing a senior honors thesis on the effect of the city block on the human personality. It was my own theory at the time that man living in wide-open spaces had a different relation to objects: because he could see where he stood, where he was going.

It was in looking back to take a bearing on my buckskin jacket, to memorize its location in order later to retrieve it, that I first noticed the magpie.

The magpie, according to my perception of relationships at that instant, was following me.

I concentrated on Miss Kundt: her proclivity for the horizontal had rendered seduction very nearly impossible. But then she noticed my eyelashes. We struck on a compromise position: she would, while staring at my eyes, levitate. She also had a theory of levitation. A theory that fascinated me, considering the difficulties I was beginning then to encounter with my own ambitions to rise in the world. She claimed that, while raised up onto my own naked body, looking at but not into my eyes, she could feel nothing, could remember nothing later of what might have transpired.

But it was not my eyelashes that moved. The sun itself was swinging. Dipping. Swinging and dipping against my eyes, the sun blurred my vision.

I looked down from the pale, cold sun to my feet. The snowshoes moved out methodically, one, then the other, before me. Under me.

But then I recognized they were not adding to the sum of my achievement. Rather, each was biting away something of what remained to me. Each step I took snipped off a fraction of the remainder: and it was then I thought of Zeno. I took great solace from the recollection of his arrow. I looked at my feet, forever dividing the space between me and my goal. I will never get there, don't worry, I told myself.

You cannot get there, a voice responded. Ever.

One of the contending voices was that of the magpie.

I had left the mere earth, you understand. I was travelling above the snow, light-footed on strange slippers. The magpie proved to be an excellent travelling companion.

Except that he would on occasion flit ahead of me, alight in the snow. He would look up and around. Then, just when I had got close enough so that we might chat again, he would take off, lightly flit on ahead.

I was no longer merely thinking. My mind was the landscape. The magpie, so neatly black and white against the sky, against the snow, was encompassed by my head. My body was totally spent. And thus I was free of my body. There was no goal now: I was following the magpie. And yet he was in my head.

We were playing a game: with a deft swerve he deluded another runner into slowing. I slipped on by. We did it again: we had mastered a trick: the magpie deluded another runner into a pause.

There was nothing left of me but my own exhaustion. The snow below us was a great bed. Only by some impossible effort could we reach it. Our straining lifted us up and outward. Away. We struggled to get down to the beautiful white sheets, the pillows of white. Which were also in my head. I could not stop the struggle downward, which took me up. Which was all in my head.

Someone was wrestling. Someone had seized me, was trying to pull me down. I was fighting to free myself. Because the magpie was escaping, was flying off, out into space. But someone, shouting, had caught me, was flinging me down in the snow.

## 30

Professor, here is one you can tell your colleagues at the next
weekly meeting of the Friday Night Mead Sippers — when you
morticians of knowledge invent your living students, over two-
for-the-price-of-one drinks and free shrimp in Ye Olde Valhalla
Bar and Grill. Tell all those exiles from Brooklyn and the Bronx.
Tell the examining committee. Tell them all that Big Sadness got
his smart-alec ass whipped for recollecting one or two dago
expressions from the streets of Little Italy.

"You see," someone was arguing, "there are runners who run
to overtake. There are runners who run to run away."

They have found me here, I thought; they have found me
collapsed, defeated, freezing in the snow; I am freezing into the
faithful oblivion of snow.

"He won," a voice was explaining. It was a professorial voice;
I was there and I was not there. "So what does it matter?"

They are laughing at me, I thought.

"That last spurt was fantastic," a voice was asserting, elabo-
rating. "This crazy bastard, he went right by me just ten yards
from the finish post. And then I had to catch up to the son of a
bitch and tackle him. I had to bring him down or he'd have gone
right on up the river and through the foothills and into the
Rocky Mountains."

I could hear, they were laughing. Someone was poking me in
the ribs. The man who claimed he had captured me gave me a
poke. "I would say he was running away," he said.

I realized we were not in the snow. I was sitting in a plastic
and aluminum chair and a group of snowshoers faced me, around
the top of a round table; each man had in front of him two
matching glasses of beer.

And then I realized why I was confused.

They looked like muskrats.

There were eight or ten sweating faces, frost-burned and sweat-burned faces, pushed together in a circle around an invisible center. But they all looked like muskrats; each face was small and curious and intent. I lifted a hand — I found my own right hand, under the table, one of two matching hands, and I lifted it, in order to pick up a glass of beer; I discovered the glass was empty. I picked up the full glass that stood at its side; I took a deliberate and measured swallow. Then the whole damned animal kingdom was crowding in on me, crowding at my mind. I remembered the kid who was a buffalo in his previous life, his two false tits full of happy dreams. I understood why he had to take the rap, no apologies, the way a buffalo walks head on into a storm. And those three princesses in their muskrat coats, trying to warm their lily-white, ice-white breasts, hugging their breasts in their arms in the blank light of day. And Bea the bear. The white old she-bear, her dugs deep-buried in fur, lovely as sin. All the tundra of the world bear-haunted and wild, the white bears prowling the mortal night.

"Stranger like this," a sweating face said. "Comes sticking his nose in here looking for trouble. Sometimes he finds it."

"Where you from?" the beak of a ski cap said, raising itself up from over a glass of foam and beer. Revealing the beady eyes of a muskrat.

Connect, I told myself. Connect.

I said nothing.

"Wouldn't be from the Hobbema Reserve, would you?"

"Maybe he just phoned from the other side of the grave and said he was on his way."

My captor raised his mouth to my ear. Lifted his shining teeth. "Dorck's woman. Communicates with the dead." He winked, then tapped at his hairy skull with his right forefinger.

"You a friend of Dorck's, ain't you?"

The funny part was, I didn't deny it. I should have said something, should have explained. I was closer to making a connection than I had ever been.

"He ran right out of himself. That happens to runners."

They were trying to understand. The heads in the centerless circle were trying to explain: and I saw then, also, they were trying to explain how they had not won. And I knew I was in trouble.

We were surrounded by tables that were surrounded by men who were drinking beer and laughing and trying to make themselves heard over the juke box. And yet there was a silence in the noise: a secret and yawning jaw behind the carousing. A cave that out of its silence made sound. I thought of a bed, a crystalline white and starch-stiff bed, around it the clocks standing still.

"Ran all right. Ran like a dog with a tin can tied to its tail."

"No." A voice was arguing with the voice. "No. He just laid back. Held back. Waited for the end. That's his goddamned little trick. Then wham. Right at the very end."

"Doesn't matter," somebody said. "What difference does it make?"

I knew I was in trouble. I wanted to start up and fly. This whole damned country, I thought to myself, they're all trying to vanish into the air. Like that magpie. Like that cowboy, a sunfishing bronco wasn't enough, he had to take flight from a catapult. And Dorck himself. Leaping, leaping, launching out over the cliff's edge, his red suit zippered against the wind, he would rise up and up and up and up —

"You part Indian or ain't you?" a voice repeated. "Just answer my goddamned question, yes or no. Or I'll judge for myself."

I saw it coming, then. I saw where I had run to. I had run right through some invisible gate, some wide and unseen gate in the endless white snow. One voice in the circle of voices had made a guess that it wouldn't give up. And when I might have explained, I saw instead the potential truth of the observation.

And then I began to understand other things, Professor. The magpie itself. The magpie looked like *you*, Madham, all dressed up in black and white. The old mad Adam of the original day. The first night, outside the garden. Kee-rist on a crutch. The grief-spinner, horned and horny in his nightmare hope, and even then, that first time, trying to recapture everything that was gone.

I looked into all the faces. I couldn't find the face that had spoken, giving the mark to my pain; but I had to tell it, had to tell one, all of them, go fuck yourselves.

"*Va fa'nculo.*" I shook my head, remembering. "*Vatte fa'fot'. Va fa'nculo.*"

"You fucking Indian," a voice said.

Why the guy hit me I'm not quite sure: but I lurched up from the table. Just that fast I had caught up the back of my chair; I raised the chair, swung, nailed him. He was wearing the chair like a helmet. But someone else was on me now. Someone jabbed, in close, and hit me below the belt. Someone else was hitting my back, trying to land a rabbit punch. I managed to jerk the chair free and I swung it again and caught someone across the forehead.

The bouncer was coming at us. He grabbed me, twisted my right arm up behind my back. Someone swung and grazed my ear.

I was smashed against a door and the door opened.

I was outside the hotel's beer parlor. It was very quiet outside, behind the hotel. The bouncer let go of my arm and turned me around. He swung at my face with a right uppercut and I ducked away. I was trying to protect my nose.

"You fucking Indian," he said. He swung again. "You come in here you want trouble, you fucker, I'll give you some fucking trouble."

I saw the blow coming.

We were standing in a square of snow, in a small space where no cars were parked. The waiting men were gathering into a circle around me. In the peculiar, glowing darkness their heads began to take on bodies.

But still they were muskrats, dark and hunched; their noses were sharp, their eyes surprised. Out of the night they came, out of the sloughs and the creeks, out of the river itself. They came from feeding. Or came to feed. They crept up from mysterious waters that I had not seen, had not ever seen, but those waters were full of lilies. Lilies frozen into the ice — and deep below the frozen surface the long stems of the lilies hung brown, hung smoothly black; in the waters where the muskrats fed the stems hung ready to enwrap, ready to ensnare the plunging swimmer.

I was at the center of the circle. Snow had begun to fall; snow was falling in the unnatural light.

The ballooning animal bodies lifted faces, raised them into a growing, dark circle. Snow fell on the figure that stepped out of the circle. Into the circle. We were facing each other. Everything was quiet.

"You an Indian or something?" a voice repeated. As if twice wasn't enough.

Again I did not answer. When I might have saved myself, simply by speaking. But I would not speak. For if I had tried, it would have been a tongue I did not understand.

In the snow, out of the falling snow, I saw the blow coming; and I saw, I realized with quiet precision, that I could not in any way avoid it. I raised my hands to protect my nose.

I could not see the face that had come to challenge me. I thought I could not see anything. Perhaps the bouncer had been there all the time, had never left the circle's center.

And then, in the night, the snow falling, in the black and white night I saw the violent clash and bloom of stars.

## 31

"They kicked the shit out of you."

I tried to nod. My neck ached as if I'd recently been hanged.

"They took you for an Indian."

I groaned.

"You look like an Indian." I recognized the voice. "You ran on those snowshoes like a streak of greased lightning."

I opened my eyes. And closed them. I was in a dirty washroom somewhere, the Cree musher and his wife were holding me upright on the toilet seat. The woman, silent and unsmiling, dabbed at my face with a wad of wet paper towels.

Maybe I passed out again.

I came to thinking about the corner of Sullivan and Houston. I remembered, and tried to forget, and remembered: a sticky hot day in the summertime, with the bigger kids playing cowboy and me being the Indian. I didn't want to be the Indian at all. They told me, You be the Indian, Sadness. We'll hunt you down. No matter where you hide, we'll hunt you down. We'll kill you. And they threw broken bricks and they tied me up and stuck lit matches into the seams of my shoes, and one time they dropped a condom full of water from a rooftop and hit my head and nearly broke my neck. They didn't mean to hurt me, they explained; they were only waiting in ambush and I happened into the canyon and they were only dropping a boulder on my head. So the tailor across the hall from my mother's apartment brought me in his books of Grey Owl; one by one, he brought them. Unfolded them. Unveiled them. He gave me his dream of the European boy who became . . . pathfinder . . . borderman . . . the truest Indian of them all.

When I was old enough, brave enough, a teaching assistantship in my bedroll, I fled Greenwich Village. Little Italy. I fled through the Catskills. Not to the wilderness. Yes, to the wilderness. To a labyrinth of streets and highways and corridors through which, in nine years, I did not learn to find my way. To a city that is not a city, but a place in the hills. Orthodox city of overcast skies and golden domes and hidden Clinton Street bars. Steamed clams at Sharkey's. Pitchers of beer in The Dive. City of green walls, rooted in stinking rivers. As you yourself remarked, Professor, every river is the River Styx. A green, lost city where a man might hide for years. Lost streets, lost rooms, lost in the forested hills. Once you are through the Catskills you are free of the east, and the east will never hold you again. But you are not yet west —

## 32

Miss Sunderman, Binghamton is surely, as a glance at any map will tell you, an eastern city, nestled though it is in a valley where two rivers meet and flow to the westward. Hurricane Agnes came to us like a vengeful woman, even as she came everywhere to the seaboard. Carol and I were trapped in her apartment — it would hardly be unfair to say, in her bed — for three days. We rode out the storm. But where was I —

From here it is an easy drive through the mountains and down to New York City. We went there, Carol and I, for a spring weekend, to see the Rangers play the Boston Bruins — and we took the trouble to look for Jeremy's much-maligned home.

We found the tall and soot-stained brick walk-up facing St. Anthony of Padua's, the old ladies dozing on their front steps, the children drinking coke at sidewalk tables. I believe it beautiful. But I am a western boy who ever dreamed east. That is my little fate.

Jeremy would make of that dozing neighborhood a frightening scene: at the drop of a hat he would conjure up games of stickball that turned into fist fights. He would recall *ad nauseam* the hot and misted passions of an endless series of crap games, in progress under the forbidden stairs; the garbage can lids that became their shields in the quick eruption of violence.

That he should have provoked some idlers into attacking him is no occasion for surprise. He had, from early childhood it would seem, a peculiar need to be trapped, cornered — more simply, to get caught.

Is it not odd, this impulse in the erring man: this need to divulge, to confess? This little need assumed immense proportions as Jeremy let himself be propelled by unconscious desires into self-revelation. To get into a corner on those vast prairies is not easy. And yet the words of self-betrayal flowed like a spring flood, like the waters from a breached dam, rolling and tossing and breaking a lost body into oblivion . . .

## 33

I opened my eyes, Professor. I tried to. I shook my head. "You threw the race," I said. To the Cree. "Why did you do it?"

"I could have won," he explained.

"No," I said. "Explain."

"I saw I could win," he explained. "After that —"

I only shook my head.

"I want to tell you," the Indian added. "They gave you a shit-kicking. They kicked the supreme piss right out of you."

I had a right to feel sorry for myself. "Why didn't somebody help me?"

"I am."

He pulled my braids forward over my shoulders; a resigned, affectionate gesture. "They left you back there behind that hotel, lying in the snow. You could have froze stiff."

"Who are you?" I asked.

"I am a Plains Cree. From the bush up north."

"I'm Jeremy Sadness." I tried to offer my hand.

He lifted my right hand and shook it. "My name is Daniel Beaver." He indicated his wife. "My wife is a Blackfoot from the plains."

We were in the washroom of the Esso station down the street to the west from the Royal Hotel. Facing the railroad tracks. Daniel Beaver explained that he had so far been unable to find a room for his wife and family. He apologized for bringing me to the washroom.

"Let me help," I said. I stood up to open the door.

"Wait," Daniel said. "You have no moccasins."

I looked down: I was in my stocking feet. The snow on my socks had melted and the beads of water were large and luminous on the wool.

"Somebody liked them," Daniel explained.

What could I do? Nothing. Where could I go? Nowhere. Chilblain and frostbite lurked outside. I was damned well lucky I could stand up at all.

"I'll go back the truck up to the door," Daniel said.

Mrs. Beaver discovered that the paper towel container was empty; she dug some almost clean towels from the waste can and got busy wiping the blood out of the greasy sink. The grease in the sink only mixed with the blood when she attempted to clean up. There was no hot water; the hot water tap didn't work. She punched some powdered soap onto the wad of towels and tried again.

Snowflakes were falling gently in the harsh light around the ESSO sign. Cars moved slowly on the street, their sound muted, their windshield wipers working against the snow. It had obviously been snowing for longer than I remembered.

Daniel carefully checked the canvas stretched over the frame on the box of the pick-up truck. He opened the flaps and rummaged inside among the dogs.

He stepped into the washroom with a jacket over his arm: a leather jacket with fringes: the golden brown Indian-tanned moosehide smells both of the tanning itself and of the dogs. On the shoulders of the worn jacket, both front and back, are floral patterns worked in bright glass beads: red and blue and yellow, black and white. But mostly a sunbright yellow.

"Can you wear this?" Daniel asked. Before I could answer he added, to assure me, "I threw it away."

There in the men's room of Notikeewin Esso they raised the old jacket behind my back, Daniel Beaver and his wife. In silence they held it up to the naked light bulb and I lifted my right arm as if I might be pointing — No. As if I might be a tree. I found it difficult to move my arms. The jacket remained suspended above me, I lifted up my left arm and stood with both arms up as if I balanced on my hands and neck an invisible world.

The jacket came down onto my hands, onto my arms. Mrs. Beaver closed the jacket zipper. She opened it and took out some dog hair and closed it again.

"Does it fit?" Mrs. Beaver said.

"It fits," Daniel said.

"It fits," I said.

I put my hands into the pockets. Only then did I realize: in throwing away my other jacket I had thrown away my ring of keys. The brass key ring itself, a gift from Miss Petcock. The Yale key to the shared office where I am scheduled this same night to embrace Miss Cohen. The Lockwood key to an upstairs apartment where, my wife being out for a visit to the professor's attic, I might let myself in to the roaring silence. The key to a friend's VW, though the friend graduated after a mere five years of earnest study and himself became a professor and a dolt. The skeleton key to Miss Kundt's levitation salon, though Miss Kundt has, in fact, since moved to another salon, yea, even another vertical lover.

The small tin key to my typewriter case. Four larger keys one of which would open a foot locker I left in storage, where, I can't recall. And a slender silver key that I could neither surrender nor, try as I might, connect with any remembered door or cash box or filing cabinet or steamer trunk or padlocked garden or chastity belt or emblazoned keyhole anywhere in the known world.

Mrs. Beaver had left us, had gone to the cab of the pick-up to where her four small sons were trying to sleep. She came back into the men's room with a pair of moccasins.

I was told to sit down again on the toilet seat. The moccasins are very old; they are decorated not with beads but with the dyed quills of porcupines. The pattern on top of the foot of each moccasin is both floral and geometric at once.

Mrs. Beaver raised up my right foot and held a moccasin upside down to the sole of my foot, to the red sock. Then she slipped that moccasin onto that foot, raised the other moccasin upside down to my other foot, was satisfied again. She would not allow me to wind the long thongs around the moosehide uppers of the moccasins. She finished tying both and then lifted up both my feet high enough in the air so her husband might examine them.

He felt very carefully the toes, the heels. "Do they fit?" he asked.

"They fit," Mrs. Beaver said. She took my hand and invited me to stand now in my new old moccasins.

"They fit," I said.

We spoke nothing more; we stepped outside, all three of us, out of the washroom and into the falling snow. I watched the flakes of snow land on my moccasins, on the shoulders of my new old jacket. We stood together at the rear of the pick-up truck.

"Where can we take you?" Daniel said.

"I must lie down," I said. "I feel queasy."

"That will be fine," Daniel said. He opened again the canvas flap that covered the rear end of the truck box. "You can climb in here with the dogs."

The smell of the dogs came out at me: it was not so much an odor as an engulfing wave. It was as if all nine dogs had breathed out together, at once.

And it was the heat of their living, the warmth, that drew me. I had to lie down. Daniel gave me a hand; I was too weak to climb into the truck box by myself. I took his left hand in my left as he helped me; that's when I felt the scar across the top of his hand.

"You hurt yourself," I said.

"When I was a boy," Daniel said. "I was setting a bear trap. The trap closed."

At that moment the canvas flap dropped shut behind me. I crouched in the straw with nine dogs: tenderly, gently, I went down onto my knees. I felt in the dark. The dogs stirred uneasily. One of them growled. I held still until the growling ceased.

"What should I do?" I whispered through the closed canvas.

"Lie down," Daniel said. He too was whispering: he might have reminded me to say my prayers. "Curl up. They will keep you warm. Where do you want us to take you?"

"What in hell," I called gruffly through the canvas, "are you doing here yourself?" I softened my voice. "What is the purpose —"

"That hill." It was the voice of Mrs. Beaver now.

Patient. Consoling. "You know that hill where the ski jump is?"

I nodded. Don't ask me why.

"Fort Duhamel was there."

I put my hand into the thick fur on a dog's back, trying to find room for myself.

"That's where it was," Mrs. Beaver was explaining. Out in the snow, outside the canvas. "The last sun dance where the fasters

105

tortured themselves to win a vision." She had finally got a chance to talk. "My grandfather was there. The pointed sticks through the muscles of his chest. The rope to the top of the pole, to the medicine bundle —"

"I wanted to tell you," Daniel called through the canvas flap. He interrupted his wife.

I was curling up into a ball. A man, perishing of cold, lost on the trail, alone and forsaken, might be saved by his team of dogs. And even as I found a place in the straw an unseen husky put down its huge jaws on top of my head and began to snore.

"Huh?" I said.

"Grey Owl would be proud."

I opened my eyes. In the total dark. I didn't dare move.

"He was a good fighter," Daniel explained. "He killed a man himself one time, in a fight."

"He killed himself," I whispered. I didn't dare flex a muscle. "He killed Archie Belaney. Then he became Grey Owl."

"I never heard of that," Daniel said. "But once he killed a man. Another man. He was quick with a knife, Grey Owl. He liked to drink. He liked women."

I didn't speak.

"He was something like you," the Indian added.

"You didn't know him," I said aloud, defending Grey Owl. No one could say those things about my borderman. My pathfinder.

"I knew him in the bush. He was brave like you. He would fight the white man." The Indian waited. I said nothing. "But when he got to town, sometimes he went wild."

Mrs. Beaver tried once again to speak. Then stopped.

"What is it?" I dared to say.

There was no answer.

"Hey," I said. Aloud. Into the husky's jaws. "Just tell me —"

There was no answer at all. The truck began to move.

## 34

I must break my silence, Miss Sunderman. Your idiot lascivious student knew *nothing*: and yet would dare to dream *my* north-west. If you understand his perverse dreaming, then you might understand my careful accounting for his end. It was earned and willed and *deserved*.

Jeremy fell asleep. He slept. God forgive him, that poor silent woman wanted to talk. She wanted to explain. It was as if she would go to confession: and he, the priest, in his cabinet, dozed off and away. Slept like a log. He was unworthy of the very dogs he slept with; but he slept nevertheless.

And yet she had her victory too, that Blackfoot woman from the plains. He dreamed her dream. "He danced himself free," Mrs. Beaver was explaining. In his dream, she had found a listener. "We wanted to see . . . we have to see . . . my grandfather . . . the buffalo were gone . . . this is a holy place, the dancers . . . waiting to hear . . . until Old Man came in, took up the buffalo stone . . . the thunder . . . distant in the hills . . . not clouds in the sky but hoofs on the earth . . . dancing . . . until the flesh . . . tore free . . ."

And the buffalo came back in his dreaming. Out of the north they came. Out of that one last corner of the Great Central Plains; from that one place where they had not all been shot and flayed. Out of Wood Buffalo Park moved twelve thousand buffalo, off the salt plains, out of the spruce forest. Moving as in a dream past the puzzled rangers. South from Salt Mountain they travelled, leaving their sink-holes and their sandy ridges. Through the forest south from the Caribou Mountains they worked their way, swimming the rivers, skirting the rapids, the beaver dams, the lakes, the falls.

The Chipewyan sent word to the Cree. The buffalo are coming back. And the long herd trailed south through spruce and

107

jack pine and tamarack and birch, through muskeg and rock. Up the Peace. Up the Wabasca valley. Skirting the Buffalo Head Hills. Up the Athabasca. Out of the Pelican Mountains. Out of the Swan Hills. Out of a dying winter.

The Cree sent word to the wondering Blackfoot: the buffalo are returning. And the great brown beasts stalked like shadows torn from the trees, out of the last green forest, into the parklands.

Now the herd was as wide as the space between the horizons. Streaming south. Out of the snow.

The buffalo calves dropped into spring, gambolled and sucked. The lean cows fed in the sloughs while frogs croaked and muskrats dove to the doors of their lodges and nesting ducks tipped down to the mud. The barbed wire fences fell rusted into the greening earth, were gone. The squared fields were hardly a trace on the burgeoning grass, on the young willows. The cowbirds fed on the backs of the shedding bulls.

The Blackfoot advised their Sarcee allies: trim the hoofs of your waiting horses. Set feathers to the arrow. Cut wood for the bow.

And the herds moved onto the bald prairies. The wheatfields were gone: the shortgrass cover of the high plains gave summer to the buffalo beans, to the blue lupine, to the pink three-flowered avens.

Tell the Bloods. The cattle are gone from the prairie ranches; the ranches are gone. Tell the Piegans. The wolves are come from the north, are waiting to eat. The grizzly comes down from the western mountains. Tell the Stonies to build the buffalo pound. Tell the squaws to gather buffalo chips. Tell the dogs to be silent. Tell the hunter to get for his medicine bundle FIRST a decorated pipestem, THEN the head of a crane, THEN a badger's skull, THEN the skin of a gopher, THEN the tail of a rattlesnake, THEN a bag of pine needles for making a smudge,

THEN a muskrat skin for wiping off sweat, THEN a bearskin, THEN a tanned elk hide, THEN the hoof of an antelope, THEN an eagle's wing-feather, THEN the foetus of a deer for tobacco pouch, THEN the skin of a grey owl, THEN a painted buffalo robe . . .

He was awakened, he didn't know how. Perhaps by the darkness itself. He might have been in a cave, the last Stone Age hunter at the end of the Great Hunt, dreaming his final prey. Thirty thousand years from Europe, east and again east, into Siberia, and again east, seeking always the great snorting bison. The horn. The hide. The sinew in the leg. The meat on the bone.

It was Jeremy's notion that two great waves of culture have washed out from Europe, one to the east, one to the west. On the Great Central Plains of America they had met again. Bloodily.

He dreamed the scalping of Edmonton. The last city north. The Gateway.

Poundmaker called his warriors to prepare their medicine. Crowfoot broke his treaty and sent out messengers: tell Sitting Bull and Crazy Horse to bring the Oglala Sioux. Tell Many Coups and the Crows to ride north. Tell the Cheyennes the buffalo are fat. And an old chief on a white horse called roll of the warrior societies:

"Notched Sticks."

"Here."

"Muddy Hands."

"Here."

"Stone Hammers."

"Here."

"Ravens."

"Here."

"Half-Shaved Heads."

"Here."

"Big-Ear-Holes."

"Here."

"Crazy-Dogs-Wishing-to-Die."

"Here."

They rode out of camp, away from the circle of tipis. Jeremy was with the warriors. He was a warrior.

He had a secret plan.

Fort Edmonton, become a city, was holding out against its own origins. Its greedy houses ate grass and trees. At the dawn of a sunny morning they took the suburbs by surprise. They galloped into the sleeping city, gave back their cries to the sudden scream.

He was resolved to save *you*, Jill, from inconvenience or captivity. Thus he was sorry when the citizens resisted. His warrior brothers had no choice but to commence the killing; and yet he was not a little surprised at their enthusiasm.

Hardly had the sun found the sky when the earth was red with fire and blood. Department stores gave up their treasures to crackling flame: banks bubbled and burst like cauldrons of molten money. Churches fell in on their weeping worshippers. High-rise apartments and their occupants, fused at last into a community of soul, smoked like wildcat gushers into the darkening sky. Lovers ran arm in arm from their cheap motels, perishing together in speaking tongues of fire. Businessmen at a conference, hand in hand, leaped together from a balcony of a large hotel, fell like a strand of dark pearls onto the indifferent cement. Drivers of automobiles, seeing the end so near, smashed their cars into poles, into trees, into plate-glass windows, into fleeing pedestrians, into each other. Rape was the order of the day for those, men and women alike, who escaped from their flaming beds. Trial by torture was the rule for those who survived the eloquent rape. Big Bear, with a handful of warriors helping, filled the local jail with uniformed policemen, then touched fire to the powder magazine; the smoking air rained badges and boots, rained ears and legs. Looking Glass found four professors and cut from each the thumb and first finger of the right hand, then asked them to lecture on truth while they bled. Crowfoot, remembering indignities of the past, captured six legislators, then forced them to scalp each other alive. A little fellow named Wolf Head cut off the testicles from a missionary and gently stuffed them into the good missionary's own mouth.

Jeremy was relieved to see there was almost no looting.

Hardly had the day begun to decline when the first buffalo drifted into what had been the city. They grazed on the rich green lawns of the old homes overlooking the river, shit all over the flower beds. They rubbed against the lamp posts and the parking meters, scratched and grunted and lay down in the shade of bloodied automobiles. They drank deep from a fountain in front of the smoking ruins of what had been City Hall. They crossed the quiet bridges, shying from the drum of their own hoofs; they chewed their cuds on the groomed grass of the bucolic campus, where the fly-touched corpses lay eyeless and open to the scoffing crows.

Jeremy was unable to locate you, Miss Sunderman, try as he might. He was certain you must have been raped in the massacre. He had believed he would save you.

Poundmaker found our hero freeing the animals from a children's zoo. Poundmaker raised his feathered spear over the head of his sweating horse. Jeremy saw the flies swing lazily in the air, around the bloodied head of the spear.

"Now," Poundmaker said, in a stern, level voice, yet in a tone that was not devoid of affection, "you are no longer Antelope Standing Still."

Jeremy was scarcely paying attention; he claims he was thinking only of your fate.

Poundmaker allowed himself a smile of fatherly pride. "Now," he said, "you are Has-Two-Chances."

It was as if the calling of the name itself awakened him. Or perhaps it was only the motion of the moving truck. But he found himself in a dark so dark he might have been in a womb. Dreaming the world to come. He was no longer a mere hunter and warrior. A green flame touched his eyes. He was reaching towards a solitary animal: a painting of a buffalo, high on a wall of stone. He could only compare it to The Bellowing Bison, that lost and discovered drawing in the holy Cave of Altamira, Spain. And then it happened.

"Professor Madham," he says, calmly, as if he had spotted me in a hallway, "I was a *buffalo* —"

## 35

The poor fucker finally flipped out. He was a buffalo's ass from the word go. Now he thought —

Jeremy was much fascinated by those Blackfoot stories of Buffalo Women — those squaws who in legend fell in love with magnificent bulls. Now, in his dream, one of those women came to him.

I need hardly point out the salient feature of this *love*-relationship: *buffalo make love standing up.*

Yes, in his dream he was not only a buffalo, he was in *love*. Love-struck and foolish as any mere mortal boy might be. Fescue and spear grass and prairie onion were all alike to him: he ate nothing. The bees sang honey in the scarlet mallow, in the yellow rays of the brown-eyed susans: he would not listen. The kit fox touched at his idle hoofs as if he might be fossil. Meadowlarks and blackbirds stole seeds away from his lolling tongue.

Then he sniffed the air. Then he walked down into a coulee, galloped straight to a saskatoon patch.

Buffalo Woman was bent to a bough that itself was bent, carried to the ground with blue-black berries. She held in her left hand a skin pail. She pretended she had not heard the pounding of his hoofs. He looked at the pail, not at the strange, familiar woman.

She had not picked a single berry.

She straightened and looked at him. With eyes that denied him. But he noticed that, unthinking, she caught in her right hand some berries, unthinking, crushed them. The berries burst in her hand and she raised her long, stained fingers to her lowering gaze. She raised her fingers to her mouth and licked with a quick tongue the blue-black berries.

She set down her pail on the parched grass.

He raised up his shaggy head, his horns. He gave out a roar that might have broken off a tree. Or cracked the stones in the river.

"Close your eyes," Buffalo Woman said.

He closed his eyes. And opened them.

As quick as that she turned herself into the most desirable buffalo cow he had ever seen.

"I am ready," Buffalo Woman said.

He sniffed the dry earth and his cold nostrils sent up puffs of dust.

"Make the earth fly up," she told him. "You must make a cloud. So they cannot see us."

He swung his horns into the matted sod. He pawed and gouged at the prairie with his hoofs and tossed up into the air the grass and the rooted clods: a cloud of dust stood over them like a tipi.

"That is enough," she said.

He reared up on his hind legs. He missed in his first lunging,

113

and fell back. Away. In a dream he was falling, and yet he did not know. He who would make a life of knowing. And he was afraid of his fall. The air was silent. The horned lark ceased its mid-air song. At the river's edge the godwits were stilled, as if the shadow of night had come to their day. The erect and squeaking flicker-tails must have dived for their holes: their presence vanished.

He reared again. He gave his piercing body into hers. And then the flourish of rhetoric was greater even than the self-born pride. They were as a storm come up in the west, he would have us believe. The crack and roll of thunder might have been less than their sudden joy. They danced the highest measure of the flesh; rocked in the cradle of all our dreaming, that cowardly lover had his moment of avail. Dreaming his advantage, he tolled the bell of his short and ethereal victory. Lumpish and swollen, he could not tell the real from the feigned. The beast imagining the beast imagining the beast. All of nature, he would let us suppose, kowtowed to the furtive whim. The sun's hot eye went stolid in the hazed air. The gusting day exploded.

The bombast of the heart, Mr. Sadness.

He let himself back to the earth. Down from her humped spine. Down from her haunches.

Buffalo Woman rubbed the thick wool of his shoulders, caressed the curve of his horns. "Yes," she said. "We will be happy. You have strong medicine."

36

I know what you will say, Madham, even before you say it. The mark of the well-trained professor. Separate and alone, Sadness, my boy. *Separate and alone*, the tragic figure of our unhappy days, embracing the shadow of his imagined self. Dreaming his universe in his own little skull. Lost in his own conniving.

Madham, let me explain something: I was not alone. I was surrounded by the jaws and assholes of nine hungry sleigh dogs. And while I was content to sleep, I was not permitted to do so. Mrs. Daniel Beaver was looking in at the rear of the truck, shaking my head by the braids of my hair. "We are here," she said.

I refused to wake up and she shook me again.

"I'm sleeping," I said. "Where are we?"

"We are at the church," she answered. "It is midnight. It is time for you to choose the most beautiful woman."

I absolutely groaned.

She was pulling me out of the truck box, out from among her husband's precious dogs, helping me down to the snow-covered ground. She is herself, I might say, no prize. It was still snowing.

"There is the door," she said.

I stared at the closed and looming door. "Come with me," I said. I should have been thanking her. I wanted to thank her for everything. Instead I said, "Please come along."

"No," she said. She was leaving. She was going to the cab of her husband's pick-up truck. "We have to look for a place to stay. Our children are weary."

"But who," I yelled after her, even as she opened the door of the truck, "is the most beautiful woman?"

Her head came up over the top of the cab. She might have been scaring buffalo into a pound. "There is a Blackfoot legend that says she is a Blackfoot." I would swear that Mrs. Beaver winked. Maybe she'd had a few beers.

The church basement door opened for me. I didn't touch it, I swear. And who was waiting to usher me into that seething cauldron of noise, sweat, carnality, venal selfishness, human ambition, vain hope, covetousness and prideful slander but Jill Sunderman.

"I knew you'd show up," she said. "I knew we could count on you."

Talk about misery in this fucking world, I wanted to die. That's all. And to be reliable is the last straw, the last trivial compliment that can be paid to a squandered life. To show up, after all, at the appointed hour. Here lies Jeremy Sadness. He was reliable to the end.

"What happened to *you*?" Jill said.

"Forget it."

"You look as if you fell off a through freight." She was staring curiously at the beadwork on my jacket. Maybe I smelled a little of dog piss. "Are you all right?"

"I'm fine," I said.

"If you're so fine, why are you scratching like that?"

I'll tell you one goddamned thing I got from those dogs, I got fleas. In that hot stinking basement they were having a burrowing contest. They were having the time of their lives. I was clawing at myself like a cowboy spurring a bronco.

A sound of grunting came to our ears.

"What's that racket?" I said to Jill.

"He was one of the winners today," Jill explained.

A guy up on the stage was calling moose. Why you would call moose in the basement of the First Presbyterian Church is one of the many mysteries I am not likely ever to fathom. My confusion only grew when he stopped. What next, I wondered. Who next? "And now," he said, "a cow moose." And then he made the strange, attractive grunts and calls that would draw a rutting bull to its death. I almost went to the stage myself.

He was roundly applauded.

"There's still time," I whispered.

"No," Jill said. She laughed her laugh of abandonment that nearly sent me running again. It bore no relation to anything we were saying. "Next the old-time fiddler who won today. Then the choosing . . . the Winter Queen."

I looked back. The way to the door was blocked by squads of muscular, granite-faced athletes, each of them spoiling to cold-cock anything that resembled a referee, umpire or judge. I looked ahead.

Even while the fiddler stomped one foot and grimaced his way through "Turkey in the Straw" — even while he chewed gum, three young women were filing onto the stage behind him, arranging themselves on three chairs that were arranged in a straight row on the left side of the stage.

I have never in my life seen three people who looked so exactly like each other as those three girls. They made the usual batch of identical triplets look like total strangers to each other. Those three princesses were within one-hundredth of an inch of being the same height. They must have been within two hours of being the same age. They were dressed in matching long white gowns and carrying identical bouquets of roses; just to insure, no doubt, that the judge would not be influenced by mere appearances.

To begin with, they were only human. Why should I choose at all?

A round of applause broke in on my dread. The audience was approving of the fiddler, I assumed. I hadn't heard a note.

Then I realized: they were not only approving of his prize-winning tune. They were delighted that the musical interlude was over. The time to choose the queen had come.

Jill Sunderman squeezed my hand. Apparently she was holding my hand. Maybe she was trying to stop me from scratching. "Look," she said.

For Christ sake they were wheeling out an empty throne into the middle of the stage. Then two husky stage hands wrestled a card table into being. They set up the card table on the right-hand side of the stage. One of them set a chair to the table.

The other placed on the table top a pencil and a pad of paper.

"That's where you sit," Jill whispered.

"On my ass," I said. "I just left this place. Didn't you notice? What are the paper and pencil for?"

"For you to take notes. Come along."

People were moving chairs so we might proceed towards the stage. The place was jammed with everything from sleeping babies to tottering centenarians. They all wanted to see the coronation.

Jill hung onto me as if I might rise up with the balloons and hide amidst the crêpe paper streamers. "Sit here," she said.

One last folding chair was unfolded for my collapse.

Jill Sunderman was up on the makeshift stage, saying something into a microphone. She was standing behind the empty throne. "I'm pleased at the big turnout . . . Roger cannot perform . . . pancake breakfast again tomorrow to support . . . I want to thank Mrs. McCleary for chaperoning . . . want to thank Mr. Rasmussen . . . thank Mr. Flanagan . . . Mrs. McGill and the church ladies . . . our visitor from New York . . . would he please . . . please come up . . . please take his . . . position . . ."

Who were they applauding? I actually looked around, waiting to see. . . . And then I remembered. Wait, I wanted to cry out. I am Has-Two-Chances. Fuck this noise . . . I was somehow both axeman and victim. I stumbled up onto the stage and nearly demolished the card table in the process of trying to get my knees under it. I seized the pencil and bowed.

A trumpet sounded. Right behind me. I nearly shit myself right there.

I fiddled with my braids to keep from scratching, and damned near got the pencil in my eye.

"Our visitor . . . is an objective and . . . disinterested and . . . is to be the final . . ."

The three maidens, the princesses, looked across the empty throne at me and all together they smiled. At me.

I mean, they didn't just bear a striking resemblance to each other. They were impeccable duplicates. They might have been Xeroxed copies of some lost original . . .

I thought of my wife, happy and content at her simple task in the Xerox Room. I remembered vaguely being married. Before I met Buffalo Woman.

I believe those three young ladies had names. I assume they had names: however, since they were perfectly well known to everyone in the audience, it was unnecessary for Jill to make further introductions. And why should I know their names? I wrote on the pad in Roman numerals: I. II. III. Then it struck me that to use numbers was to prejudge. I crossed them out. Having commenced writing, I tried to record something more on the pad. For appearance, sake.

Judge Sadness, I wrote. Then I noticed the pun. I crossed it out.

I drew a picture of a prick and balls, the prick pendant. Quickly I turned the pad end for end. The illusion didn't work. I transformed the prick into a Christmas tree.

Dissertation Number Eight, I wrote. Colon. Blank.

The three young ladies had commenced the ritual. They had seen it performed so often in the past they had no need to be told now what to do. And why should I know what they were doing?

I was the only goddamned stranger within 500 miles of that stage. Trust my luck.

Those three mysteries were carrying roses that were peculiarly orange and purple in the blazing lights, the bright blossoms themselves almost lost in green leaves. Quickly I scratched on my pad: RED YELLOW BLUE.

Miss Red stood up from her chair and arranged her hands under her bosom. Her bosoms. Which is it? She smiled, walked along the apron of the stage directly at me, smiled again, turned around, eased her hips into motion, walked along the apron of the stage, sat down again.

The thunder of applause. Goddamn. Whoopee. Look at that.

Miss Yellow arose and did likewise. The crowd loved it. My despair grew. Hooray. Thunder of applause.

It was a problem in the angle of perception. The audience had a view of each candidate in profile, of motion across the field of vision; a horizon and a foreground united by a common pursuit. But the candidates were coming straight at me, then moving straight away. I was getting no depth into the picture. I was trapped into my own tight focus on that which zoomed in, retreated. Under the heading of Dissertation Number Eight I wrote: The Forgery of Distance: Ritual for a Long Night.

Miss Blue commenced her activity. Frantically I wrote in acute summary on my pad:

STOOD.
SMILED.
WALKED.
SMILED.
TURNED.
WALKED.
SAT.

Wow-eeee. Goddamn. Ear-piercing whistles of sheer abandon. Thunder of applause.

Not once did any one of the candidates speak a word. Not a human word. To me, a man forever attracted to the maelstrom. Something in me wanted to write in the margins of those lives: Awk. Frag. Emph. Cap. Fig. Instead: I was offered silence. What in heaven was I supposed to judge?

I tore the first page off my pad, crushed it in my fist and hurled it backstage. I drew three vertical lines down the second page, making four columns. In the lefthand column I wrote Teeth. I made a check in each of the three columns. Hair. Check check check. Ear Lobes. Check check check. Nostrils. Check check check. Jaw. Check check check. Elbows. Check check check. I began to suspect I had launched myself into an endless task. I extended my original three vertical lines to the bottom of the page. Knuckles. Check check check. Sooner or later, one variation would have to show up. Ankles. Toes. Vertebrae. Intestines small and large. Pancreas. Kidneys. Check check check check check check. Cunt. Supposing that the profligacy of nature had not gone into decline. Check check check.

The latter proposition set me to thinking. The human impulse to meditate. I could see that Jill was delaying the candidates, waiting for me to catch up with my note-taking. I had somehow to sort the potential winners in my mind. I hit on a magnificent idea: I would unite each one with a recollected woman of more intimate acquaintance. A variation on the imprint theory. The baby chick taught to love a cardboard box or the rat that would eat it.

I nodded to Jill. She nodded to the candidates. One of them stood up again, walked only as far as the center of the stage; and there she produced, as if by magic, a mouth organ.

I tried to think back on the charms of Miss Cohen, her tits like the Grand Tetons, her A paper on passion. A strange thing. My memory failed me: the most intimate details were blanched from my watery mind. I switched hastily to Reggie, to punish myself into more acute awareness. Ordinarily just the thought of her name would make me smell chocolate.

Nothing.

Stale, stale, oh custom doth stale, I told myself: go back, farther back, deeper down.

121

I glanced around at the hushed audience there in that church basement: I was reminded of a Miss Petcock who worked in the library of the State University of New York at Binghamton, a young lady who wore short skirts, very short skirts, and who, one morning, showing me how to use a microfilm reader in the basement of the library, yielded, even there, up against the reader that she had only then switched on, to the darkest dimension of our mutual lust.

No details. I could not summon up the distinguishing details. Yes: she gave me in fond memory a brass key ring.

IT WAS ALL ONE BIG FUCKUP.

Frantically I tried to remember a secretary I screwed only once, and then briefly; she was typing my fourth dissertation for me; it was late at night in the Library Tower, we were correcting some misnumbered footnotes, the bats or nighthawks fed on the moths in the bastard light outside our naked window . . . but no. Nothing so good as Buffalo . . . I remembered Carol. At dawn in an empty sculpture garden, up against a twisted beech tree that tumbled its odd shape against a waning moon; she was a virgin then; we were young, unmarried, happy —

It all broke in on me. I was giddy with fright and hope. Remembering. The errors, the faults, the miscalculations. Every peccadillo and blemish and vice that might excuse me, disqualify me, bar me from ever judging anything ever again. Me, assigned once more to throw the first stone, the stone gripped firmly in my right hand. Booze, I thought, booze: two hundred six-packs per annum bombasting the mind. Insufficient, the voice said. You are not excused. Faulty perception and compounded errors in judgment, a mere scratching of the crotch at age two years four months leading to seduction, rape and white slavery. Insufficient, the voice said. You are not disqualified. Learning to read. Insufficient. Dreaming a dream. Insufficient. Hoping. Insufficient.

The colossal failures of my own clay feet. The unmitigated disasters unmitigated. You are not barred. The constant ravening of the flesh and the eager departure from final reason. The peccant peccancies of the pecker.

EVERYTHING IS A MISTAKE.

The girl playing the mouth organ was playing the mouth organ. Beyond that I could decide nothing. I assume she was playing the mouth organ.

She stopped.

The crowd simply went wild. I recognized right then that should I make the wrong choice, that same crowd would quite simply lynch me. Chain me to its feverish joy.

On my pad I wrote: I want to go home.

Miss Yellow — or was it Miss Blue? I was now confused as to who had originally sat in which chair; the chairs were exactly alike — now rose up and walked to the center of the stage. She did not produce a mouth organ.

She was, apparently, reciting a poem. Or casting a spell on the audience. She did not raise her voice enough so that any mere mortal might hear. Her lips, however, were moving. Yes, I am persuaded it was the recitation of a poem that occupied her: at one point she gestured. Perhaps she was making a speech. Perhaps she was quoting for us a moment in our political life that changed the course of all man's travail. Ha. But no; I resolved finally that the moment was poetic. A soliloquy was being recollected from her own happier childhood. A carefree day in school when she memorized, for the pure love of sound and sentiment, four hundred lines from a dead author.

It was quite a long recitation. I had time to develop a theory of beauty. If I have failed the stern practical test, I told myself, then let me come up with a generalization that will deliver future generations out of my dilemma. Beauty, first of all, is . . .

On my pad I wrote in large letters: BUFFALO WOMAN.

To say that the crowd was once again pleased would be an understatement. I had secretly decided on the basis of applause alone that Miss Red was the winner. Now it seemed obvious that Miss Yellow — or Miss Blue if I was mistaken about the chair — was every bit as good.

The remaining contestant — at least I assume it was not the first one again — now rose from where she was seated and removed herself to the center of the stage.

I could not, from where I was sitting, see what occupied her; but I would gather from the response of her admirers that she was engaged in some not insignificant act of sleight of hand. She produced — and I could see that she produced it from her bouquet — an egg.

What does one do with an egg on a Thursday night in the basement of the First Presbyterian Church, after one has produced it? I began to worry for the poor girl. Human sympathy crept in to my considerations. The little bitch fooled me. Just as I was beginning to doodle, she made the egg vanish. Clean out of sight. She bowed. The crowd had its usual paroxysm.

You won't believe the third and final round in that contest unto death or victory. The trio stood up together, marched to the center of the stage together. Somewhere, behind a curtain, someone began to play a piano.

And the three contestants began to sing.

TOGETHER.

Yes. They were singing together, the three of them. And I was supposed to pick out the winner.

They have magnificent voices. Perfect. No exaggeration can do justice to the beauty of their singing: harmony was restored to its rightful place in the universe. The stars moved according to a heavenly edict. Those three girls who had been bored, distracted, uneasy, awkward, clumsy, embarrassed, mousy, depressed: they were suddenly beautiful. Their faces lit up the whole basement: they were genuinely, honestly happy. I was happy. We were all happy. A number of people were clapping their hands with the singing. I gave my own hands a little clap and people were pleased.

Only then I noticed something.

Here and there, in the crowd, eager faces were no longer watching the glorious trio.

They were watching me.

And then I guessed it.

The time had come. After the contest, the final song.

I WAS ABOUT TO NAME THE QUEEN.

Assuming she had a name.

I reviewed the alternatives to the act of choosing and found I had none. My initial impulse was to seek consolation in the concept of death, that unlikely hypothesis so fatally attractive to minds as finely discriminating as my own. The idea, however, would not hold; it was preposterous beyond words. Next I cast myself upon the tempting notion that I was not judging, but rather, being judged. Those sirens had sung me to my own disaster. They were testing *me*. They were putting me to the sword's point, to the post in the middle of the woodpile.

And then the shadow of a truth fell like a club: I recognized that a man who is not susceptible to bribery is not fit to be judge. He lacks the human touch.

I looked at those singing innocents, entreating any one of them to offer me the smallest bait. Even as I held the pencil transfixed above paper I was imagining the price and toll. And I was listening. Miss Red, if she was Miss Red, sang me the offer of safe passage home. I was nodding when I heard another voice: By dawn tomorrow. Wait. Wait, said the second voice. But say me queen and I'll bring your dissertation. Number Nine: The Terrors of Completion. On excellent bond. With the proper margins.

My soul's debate was ferocious. When over the halloo came the third voice, crooning me the offer of a job. Name the post you wish and the wish shall be sire to the fact. This young gentleman, of superb credentials and impeccable character, would be a fine catch . . .

And after disaster: catastrophe. The song in my own head singing No. I wanted none of their bribes. I could not take any bribe that I was capable of imagining.

I knew no name that I could call.

The music had stopped. My time had come.

I wanted to shout aloud: By comparison with Buffalo Woman, you are all faithless.

What could I do?

My right arm, holding aloft the pencil, was paralyzed. It would take a whole hospital just to set one finger into motion. The fleas eating at my balls might have been offering a caress; I could not budge a protesting hand. All of me ached. From running. From being struck. From freezing in the snow. From sleeping with a pile of stinking dogs. Movement itself was ruled out as a possibility, an obsolete concern of the dead past. I knew what I needed: I needed my tape recorder. I needed to whip out the mike, press the buttons. . . . Should I live to retrieve it I would never again let it out of my protective embrace . . .

The silence in that basement was almost more than I could bear. Suddenly my mind was a riot of possibilities. A debate was going on in my motionless skull.

THEY ARE ALL WINNERS.

There is always a loser.

THEY ARE ALL LOSERS.

There is always a winner.

126

I GIVE UP.

So give up.

I CAN'T GIVE UP.

It was then some goddamned invisible fool sounded that god-damned tinny trumpet again. I shit myself.

Professor, I speak metaphorically.

I found myself unable to groan.

It was then that a cap trimmed in wolverine, the smell of Sen-Sen, an old man, leaned over my shoulder. Where he had come from I can't imagine. He was whispering:

"It's all fixed, you dumb asshole."

"What do you mean, it's all fixed?"

"Who's going to win. It's all fixed beforehand."

"Well who the hell won?"

"I forget."

"You can't forget."

"I was never told."

"This is an outrage." I could feel a twisted grin come over my face, threatening to wring tears out of my eyes. "Those poor girls have gone through the misery of endless competition. They've paraded and performed for this mob of fanatical baboons. I'm going to pick a winner if I get hanged for my effort."

"You can't," the old man insisted. I recognized him suddenly; I had seen him watching me in the curling rink. "You're a figure-head," he explained. "You're not supposed to judge."

"Well who won?" I said. Resigned.

"They sell tickets. The person who gets the most buyers is the winner."

"I REPEAT," I whispered, "WHO WON?"

"Mr. Dorck keeps the records," the old man said.

You won't believe me, Professor. The mention of that man's name gave me an idea.

I stood up. I struggled out from under that goddamned collapsing card table, seized up my tablet, walked over to where Jill was waiting behind the empty throne. I took the microphone out of her hand. A great calm washed over me. I looked out at the huge, the waiting audience. The audience heaved a communal sigh. I looked down at the pad in my hand.

On the pad I read: I want to go home.

Under that I read: BUFFALO WOMAN.

"Ladies and gentlemen," I began. "This has been a rare opportunity for me. First of all I want to thank all of you for making it possible. I know the three young ladies are each of them a pearl beyond price."

I held the microphone away from my mouth. "Jill," I said. Loud enough so that she might not refuse. "This will take some time. Please sit down while I talk." I signalled her into the throne.

She was tired from standing so long, from her busy day; she sat down. With a small, unearthly laugh. The whole audience broke up; they laughed along with her. She crossed her legs and laughed again.

"As all of you know," I continued, "the true king of this annual festival has always been Mr. Roger Dorck."

Shouts of approval. The strong winds of applause.

"As you all know," I went on, "our king this year has been struck into an awful silence. He has fallen from a hill. His injury cannot be determined by all the knowledge of our medical science; and all the skills of that same science have not yet brought back to us his voice and his judgment."

A great wave of sorrow washed over the assembly. They were hushed into awe, those raised faces. I waited. I might have heard a pin drop, a wing fold.

I turned now to a woman whom I could see waiting behind a

curtain; the chaperone, presumably. I beckoned to her and said in a soft voice that was yet loud enough for all to hear, "Bring in the crown, please."

Necks craned; faces came forward to be witness. An elderly woman walked sternly across the stage and delivered to me the silver crown: the spiked cardboard circle bore around its rim in crayon and ink a band of flowers I could not name.

Someone had hastily made a crown. As if the victory itself had been sudden, unexpected. I stood behind the throne, holding the microphone in one hand, the crown in the other.

"Ladies and gentlemen," I said. "And boys and girls and little children. It is not for me to doubt the perfection of each of the waiting princesses. But this year, as you all well know, the success of the festival has been, is, and will be due to none other than the king's own princess." I hesitated, raising the crown over the throne. "And therefore, my dear citizens, I would like, with your consent, to crown her this year's — Winter Queen."

It was a bastardly thing to do, I suppose. I set the silver crown on the head of Miss Jill Sunderman. Scapegoat and martyr. Through no fault of her own. Before she could protest she was regal to the eye; a roar of approval came up from the startled audience. A great huzzah. They were shouting, yes. And applauding.

But they were weeping too. Don't ask me why.

The people in the crowd were weeping. Old women wept, and children, kneeling on their benches to see. The three matching princesses were weeping together. I was weeping. We were all very happy. I was surprised myself at what I had done.

Jill Sunderland was wearing the crown. She sat straight with her legs crossed, her arms on the arms of the throne. She was wearing a strange smile.

"Long live the Queen," I blundered, to her admirers.

She took the microphone from my hand.

She flicked the microphone off and raised her mouth towards me and I bent to listen.

"You are a useless prick," she said.

"I had no choice," I explained. I gave a broad smile to the admiring audience, and I nodded.

"How could you resist crowning yourself?"

That remark did it.

I was staring at Jill where she sat on her throne. But looking at her, at the beautiful blonde crowned queen of winter — God forgive me, I thought of Jeremy Bentham. Jeremy *Bentham*. The ultimate professor. It was too much altogether. That ultimate crowned head of professorhood. He who would give a grade to justice, pleasure, law, luxury, will, duty, ambition, honor, pain, belief, fiction, chaos . . .

I knew I had to get out of there.

Jill had flicked on the microphone. "My dearest subjects," she was saying, regal and sure, "let us now clear the chairs and the benches from the floor. Tell the players to bring up their instruments. We will dance until dawn."

I wanted to dance, let me tell you. Just once in my goddamned fucked-up book-spent life, I wanted to dance clean through the night: damn the unwritten papers. Damn the forthcoming exam.

I left through a fire exit.

## 37

Miss Sunderman: The sort of emotional anxiety your hero was experiencing, we are led to understand, is not uncommon in frigid climates. The phenomenon sometimes described as arctic hysteria has been examined by a number of Russian authorities, especially Krivoshapkin and Vitashevsky — though in all fairness I should add that a Mr. Eliade disputes their conclusions. The extreme cold, the long nights, the solitude of *unbounded space*: these are the enemies that induce that northern ecstasy. I had hoped to send you a copy of Ohlmarks, *Studien zum Problem des Schamanismus* — but I cannot find an adequate translation. At any rate, the afflicted person, quite commonly, senses the presence of another who is not in fact there. Mr. T. S. Eliot, to take a literary example, attributes the experience to the members of Shackleton's Antarctic Expedition: those explorers, at the edge of exhaustion, were deluded into believing there was amongst them *one more member* than could actually be counted.

I happen to know something about cold weather — perhaps I have mentioned as much. I know the effects of a Great Plains winter. Your Jeremy, growing up in the east, felt compelled to play Indian; I can only assure you I have been Indian enough. I prefer to forget the experience, and yet I do recollect the sense of being — how shall I say? — *trapped* in the blank indifference of space and timelessness. And I would insist it was just that — the pressure not of time, but of its absence — that horrified those brave men who stumbled onto the central plateau of Antarctica. Jeremy, in his own confused and piddling way, had strayed into a like circumstance, a like experience. He records as much.

A full-scale blizzard was blowing when he emerged from the church basement. There is something exhilarating about a snowstorm: I confess to receiving a certain sexual impetus from that natural — so to speak — paroxysm: but then I suppose I am a natural man. The driven fragments of ice both brace and abrade the skin; the snatching wind stiffens the resolve. One rises to the occasion.

Jeremy only reflected that he had had enough of what he

called "sobriety"; he wondered where he might find "the drinking crowd" on such a night.

<h2 style="text-align:center">38</h2>

His loneliness and isolation drove him through the snowchoked streets of Notikeewin. He found, by accident it would seem, the Corner Drugstore; he went up the narrow stairs. The door to the office of Roger Dorck, Barrister and Solicitor, was not locked. He let himself into the deserted office. Into the deserted three-room apartment behind the office.

He felt an urgent need to find his lost, his abandoned, suitcase. He does not say why. Surely not to work on his dissertation. I suspect he had recognized his own shadow: he wanted, once more, to run.

And then the old disaster recovered its missing victim.

Where he had expected to find his suitcase, he found instead his tape recorder.

Consequence: he seized the recorder in his shaking hands. He jerked the microphone out of its leatherette pouch. He pushed the plastic buttons, listened for the first whisper of the turning tape: TESTING, TESTING ONE TWO, TESTING THREE FOUR FIVE SIX SEVEN EIGHT NINE . . .

He talks. He jumps to his feet and falls down on the floor on his toes and fingers and one UP two UP three UP four UP five. He talks some more. He does his grip exercises: open the right hand, stretch the fingers, make a fist; open the left hand, stretch the fingers — get that thumb back — make a FIST goddamnit, close that hand as if you are going to CATCH something; open your right hand. . . . He talks. He exercises. He talks. He exercises. He talks.

A knock comes at the office door.

"Come in," he shouts.

The knock is repeated.

"COME IN," he shouts.

## 39

Two hooded figures are standing outside the door in the dark hallway. They are absolutely covered in snow. White, in snow, in the dark hallway.

One of them points to the other.

The other speaks: "We cannot find you a bed."

"A bed? I don't need a bed. What the hell do I need a *bed* for?"

"Mr. Sadness, sir," the first one explains. "We cannot *find* you a bed. Because of the blizzard."

"I don't fucking need a fucking bed. Do you hear me?"

"We'll do our best, sir. Come along now."

## 40

Professor, you will no doubt presume to recognize in these two figures the devil's tragic doormen, or some such obscenity. Some pompous integument of your own enduring death-wish. They were *in fact* two kind gentlemen detailed by the Winter Queen to find beds for all marooned travellers. They were also, I should add in all fairness, pissed right out of their skulls. They led me down the stairs, unquestioned, unquestioning, and into the storm.

We were out in the street, leaning against the wind. You might lie down at an angle, on that wind, and let yourself be swathed in snow. We hardly proceeded; and yet we would do so, or perish in our vast attempt.

We turned the corner by the Royal Hotel: a snowplow had heaped up snow around the ice buffalo and the Indian with the bow and arrow. His horse was galloping belly-deep in snow. The trapper behind the dogsled was driving a team that had disappeared into a drift. He carried on unperturbed.

"We need a drink," one of my captors said.

"After we find a bunk for our friend," the other insisted.

The first speaker raised the bottom of his parka and brought out of his hind pocket something he referred to as a micky. It proved to be a small flat bottle full of rye whiskey. We emptied it.

We were standing under the banner announcing this February festival, hunched together, introducing ourselves, when I noticed a much smaller sign. One I had missed on the night of my arrival.

Beside the main door of the railroad station is a brass plaque:

John J. Backstrom MLA
FUNERALS ARRANGED

Someone had turned the old station into a blood-red funeral parlor. A funeral home.

So what did we do?

We shook hands, nodded to each other, turned all together, and barged in through the marked door, jostled each other as if we must be in some great hurry.

A party was in progress. I am slightly taller than average, Professor, slightly taller than you, and as far as I could see, people were raising glasses to their mouths. Lowering glasses. Moving their mouths. Raising and lowering glasses and moving their lips. It might have been a dance of some sort, a strange beckoning and greeting and denying. The room was full of mouths. They gave out a steady din, a drone: no voice was to be distinguished from any other voice, no laugh was more or less a laugh than any other. The sound was never quite human. I could, in some deafening way, hear nothing, and I was frightened.

"Let's find the registration desk," Sonny Sunderman said. Shouted.

134

I should explain that one of my hosts was the father of the vanished Robert Sunderman. He is a very old man. Seems very old. He knocked the snow off his parka hood, off the shoulders and arms of his parka. He lowered the hood, pushed it back, and under it was a cap trimmed in wolverine fur, the smell of Sen-Sen.

He led the way now, pushing, easing a path among bodies that seemed to be living plants in a current of moving water. Elbows retracted gracefully. Hips swayed forward, eased forward, in some invisible and yet erotic design. Glasses seemed to elevate each other into safety. We found ourselves, judging by the overhead pattern of crêpe paper streamers, at the center of the huge room.

The spot was occupied by a mauve-colored, oak-trimmed coffin. Under the closed coffin was a set of wheels; on top was a variety of bottles, empty glasses, containers of ice.

There was, curiously, a circle of empty space around the bar. A ring. We stepped into that ring.

"Scotch and soda, anyone?" Digger inquired.

His nickname derives from the simple fact that he is the local gravedigger. I assume this to be the case; if he has another name, I did not ever hear it. He had spent the whole day digging a grave and had never been told for whom.

Digger is a close friend of the owner of the establishment, and immediately he set himself at ease. Carefully, intently, he poured three strong drinks. We raised each a full glass and said each to the other, "Here's looking at you."

A stranger, his back to us, without looking around replied, "Here's mud in your eye."

I drank my drink down to the bald ice cubes. Digger took my glass and began to mix me another generous drink. "What'll it be?" he said, pouring scotch over the ice cubes in the glass.

"The same," I said.

Sunderman was also being very serious. "I'll explain to

someone," he said, "that we stand in need of a bed."

"Certainly," I said. I drank down into my second drink.

"Let me handle this," Digger said. At that same moment he spied a desk only a few feet away; the press of the crowd had kept it from our view. He signalled us to follow and gently we moved, in his wake, over to the desk.

"Excuse me," he shouted.

The stooped, greying figure at the desk looked up from his typewriter; he had been watching very closely the line of type he was typing. "I'm almost finished," he said. He bent again to the typewriter and began to type furiously. We, the three of us, watched intently as he bent and closely watched what he was typing.

"What can it possibly mean?" Sunderman burst out. He who had given a son to vacancy itself.

"Shhh," Digger said. He raised a finger to his lips. He had not removed the parka hood from over his head and it wasn't always easy to follow his instructions.

I emptied my glass.

"There," the man said, raising his head again. He had eyes that were almost green.

"I'm trying to find a bed for this visitor." Digger indicated me where I swayed in a kind of circle around the glass I managed somehow to hold still in my hand.

"I'm sorry." The man who had been typing shook his head as if in genuine despair. "Most of the people here," he explained, "will have to stay awake all night. They'll be offered empty beds in the morning."

"I can't do it," I said. "I've got to sleep."

Actually, I don't know why I was suddenly exhausted.

"Is there no place where he could lie down?" Digger insisted.

"I'll have to go get Mr. Backstrom," the typist said. "A prince among men," he added to himself, then stood up. He vanished at an instant into the crowd. Taking his chair with him.

Digger turned away from where the chair had been and took the empty glass out of my hand. He went to the bar and began again to mix me a drink. Then he mixed another drink for Sunderman, another for himself.

The three of us raised our glasses. "Here's looking at you," we said. We each drank deeply.

"Perhaps," Digger said, indicating the bar, "you could rest briefly in this coffin."

"That would be adequate," I said.

Digger then indicated to two men who were filling their glasses that they must give a hand at moving the bottles and the glasses and the ice. They agreed at once and the three men began to transfer bottles from the top of the coffin to the nearby desk. Other people began to help. Sunderman stood rooted at my side. I commented once, briefly, on the glazed surface of his eyes.

When the lid of the coffin had been cleared, Digger lifted it open. The men who had helped him clear it went back to their drinks and their various conversations.

"Can you make it?" Digger said.

"I should take off my moccasins," I said.

"That's up to you," he said.

I tried to bend down to untie my moccasins and found that on bending over I had a tendency to pitch forward.

"Let me hold your drink," Sunderman said. He took my drink.

"Get in," Digger said. "I'll take off your shoes after you get in."

Digger guided me into the coffin. He tried to guide me in. In fact, I got in by making a kind of jump, the kind of roll a pole vaulter makes as he goes up and over. I made a very deft turn and found myself lying on my back in the coffin.

Digger was trying in vain to unlace my moccasins when the

typist returned with a huge man who put a hand on my forehead.

Introductions were made.

"Backstrom. Sadness. Sadness. Backstrom."

We shook on it.

"You saving this one for Mr. Dorck?" Digger inquired.

Mr. Backstrom gave out a huge laugh. "First come, first served." Then he pointed a huge finger between Digger's eyes. "What would kill that fucker Dorck?"

Digger only winked in rebuttal. "We've never lost a customer yet."

On that reminder, Mr. Backstrom looked into the coffin and studied me for length and fit. At the same time I studied him: he is a big bull of a man, too tall for his own cheapskate coffins. He wears grey sideburns. "Are you comfortable?" he inquired.

I complained of thirst.

Sunderman returned my glass and I raised my head awkwardly so I might take a drink.

"Just for one night," Digger explained. "He'll pay when he checks out."

Mr. Backstrom arranged the satin under my head. "We might have to give him notice. Should I get a call —"

"Of course, of course," Digger agreed, accommodating and reasonable.

Sunderman took the glass out of my hand. I was spilling it. "I think you've had enough," he said. "Excuse me for saying so." He bent close to me. "My son never took a drink."

"Never touch it myself," I responded.

"Robert. Wouldn't drink. Picture of health."

He was talking about his son. Who wouldn't take a drink. Who drowned. Who might have drowned. The best damned hockey prospect this country ever produced. Who might have phoned from his watery grave.

138

"The Rangers were scouting him. Offered him a contract. . . . You from New York, ain't you?"

There I was, being quizzed again. Examined.

"I am."

"Guess you've seen the Rangers play."

I told a lie. I had to tell one small lie. "Sure," I said. "They're pretty good. Hadfield. Stemkowski. Ratelle."

Old Sunderman allowed himself a radiant smile. "Learned to play on a frozen slough, Robert did. Wouldn't do a day's work on that dried out, hailed out, gumbo homestead of mine, couldn't stand the sight of a field of wheat. But let the first slough freeze over in the fall, he was out there on his skates, chasing a frozen horse turd with a willow stick."

I nodded. I tried to nod.

"Had the perfect physique for hockey. For a forward, not defence." Old Sunderman was staring straight through me; through me and the coffin. "Never found hide nor hair of my boy."

Mr. Backstrom, out of habit I suppose, took my wrist and felt my pulse.

"That fucker Dorck happen to die," he said to Digger, "be a blessing for all of us."

"At least he could afford it," Digger said.

"Strong as an ox," Mr. Backstrom said. Letting go of my wrist. "I'll be stuck with a second-hand coffin."

His roar of laughter attracted a couple of drunks who came over to look at me. "Hey," one of them said. "Ain't you supposed to judge that beauty contest?" He had, obviously, lost a few hours in the course of his merrymaking. He bent close to my right ear in the coffin. "You're free, white and twenty-one, ain't you?"

I tried to nod.

"What do you care who wins?"

I tried to shake my head.

"If a few dollars would help you choose . . ."

I guess I fell asleep at that moment.

I confronted a whole damned graveyard full of tombstones. The modest, grey stones were in a graveyard that was being buried in drifts of snow. I looked at one of the inscriptions and mouthed the words:

JEREMY SADNESS
Too Good For Earth
God Called Him Home

Embarrassed by that untoward praise, I hurried on to another marker. I kicked the snow away from the almost buried stone. Bent eagerly. Only to read this time:

JEREMY SADNESS
At Rest
At Last

For all the implied compliment, I was still made uneasy. I studied the multiplying stones as if each was a riddle that might cost me my life. Fear presented me with the illusion of alternatives: I looked and recognized on the boundary of the closing storm, more and still more stones. I selected one at random, moved towards it:

JEREMY SADNESS
Died of Apoplexy
While Conceiving
His 10th Diss:
The Theory of Consequence

I must in all honesty admit that it felt good to see my name in print. Professor Madham, I thought to myself, this spendthrift gardener has multiplied my fame. I am granite-hard in my immortality. No tape will equal this.

I was father to that abundance. And father-like I stooped to one of my progeny.

The stone of my most careful choosing read:

JEREMY SADNESS
Arise

The jest and mockery were too much. I awakened: I woke up and at first was quite unable to open my eyes against the light. I lay very still, trying to take account of where I might be and what was going on. Perhaps the first thing I noticed was the noise: there was a roar of conversation that sounded like a waterfall. I might have fallen asleep in a forest by a stream, with green ferns shading my head, the balm of spring water cooling my tired feet. And then I heard the music. I listened very hard and I was able to recognize an accordion and a guitar. That's good, I told myself, at least here they use musical instruments that I'm familiar with. That assured me. Then I recognized the sound of feet shuffling on a floor. People were dancing. I sensed in my shoulders and the back of my head that the floor was yielding ever so slightly to the weight of people moving rhythmically together. I lay still, letting the sense of motion seep into my shoulders. Letting it touch the back of my head. A mortal thought came into my mind: I swallowed. It seemed in my head that I had swallowed the sensation of swallowing. While doing so I blinked, though my eyes were already shut. I tried that again. I blinked quickly with my eyes shut.

Then I blinked my eyes open and shut them again.

Someone had placed two tall candles at the head of the coffin. Some smartass. It was the light of the candles that made me close my eyes. I kept my eyes shut and thought again: thinking down to my chest now. I recognized that it was rising and falling. That reassured me also. I lay so still and thought so hard that I was able to take my pulse by feeling my heart within my chest.

141

It was definitely beating. Damn the candles, I blinked my eyes open again. I kept them open, just barely cracked open, for a moment.

Sunderman was standing beside the coffin; standing at attention, silently watching something. Not me. Something beyond us. His eyes were glassy and as fixed as the eyes of an owl.

I noticed that the music had stopped. Lying in my cocoon of noise I was able to concentrate very intensely on my own silence. I was able to feel the blood running in the veins in the crook of my left arm. In my mind I followed down inside my left arm to my hand, to my slightly crooked fingers. I counted them from inside. Then, in my mind, I made a wild leap across my body to my other hand. I tried to make the leap. But I discovered that my hands were joined. I thought very intensely about all my fingers and realized that someone had folded them together. They were intertwined. They must be resting on my chest, I decided.

What happened next is very important.

I thought about my hands and then realized they were not folded on my chest but rather on my belly. On my slight beer gut. I thought about my folded hands. I thought about my belly. Then I thought down through the thicket of my own pubic hairs.

And for a moment I flinched rigid.

I had a hard-on. Yes. I was lying down, lying flat on my back. I must be dreaming, I thought. I thought again. No, definitely, I could feel my prick straining against my levis. I was not dreaming.

And then I thought, good God, I'm lying here exposed while hundreds of people look at me. They're lined up —

I had to peek.

Carefully, slowly, I tilted my head up off the satin. Carefully I opened my eyes.

At first I saw nothing. The two candles at my head gave a guttering light. I could see my own eyelashes. Then I looked hard, peeking, and I realized I could not see my own body for a very good reason.

I was buried in flowers. Some clown had absolutely filled the coffin full of roses. I expected to see my prick rising through the leaves and blossoms and thorns and crowned in laurel. Whatever the hell laurel is. But no, I had not been exposed. I closed my eyes and exulted. I tightened the muscles of my belly and felt the new tension on my zipper. I was alive. I was alive, goddamnit, I was back in the game, rearing to go, lusting to paw the dirt and snort a little.

Lying there, thinking, rejoicing, I began in my mind to write myself a letter of recommendation. TO THE PROSPECTIVE EMPLOYER, I began: Dr. J. Sadness, PhD, has been a close friend of mine for many years, both as an academician and as a warm human being, and I can testify that, yes, he is a man of exceptional talent and energy, but more than that, he is a man whose talents and energies continue infinitely to blossom and grow. He is superbly trained. He is a master of thrust and sally in the classroom. His dissertation, recently published, is certain to set the intellectual community on its ear and will probably force a re-evaluation of all that has been thought and said on — Colon. Blank. His one drawback, and surely it is a small one, is his outrageous and eternal horniness. Rumour has that he once screwed the beautiful Professor Mabel Fenn of the Biological Sciences in the campus greenhouse, up against the potted —

And then my absolute joy was united inextricably with the usual unmitigated despair.

Of course I could get a hard-on while lying down. Any time I wanted to. All I had to do was climb into a coffin. In a crowded room in a raging blizzard. With a party in progress.

It would not be the easiest circumstance to duplicate at a moment's notice. Explain this to your wife. I've taken a job at the North Pole, dear. And the memo from the Executive Vice-President: Why the coffin in your office, Mr. Sadness?

Climb in, Miss Cohen, we are going to try it flat out for a change.

I was careful not to flex a limb or make a motion. The room all about me had fallen silent.

Then a voice on the silence announced: "And now it is time. Time, everyone. For the coronation. For the crowning blow."

Followed by gales of laughter that threatened to crack the floor beneath me.

Without thinking, unable to check myself, I tilted my head and opened my eyes. For an instant I saw an opening in the crowd.

Three girls in white were coming towards me. The three ladies-in-waiting in long white gowns. They made up a stately procession; and they carried, the three of them together, a crown that was a dunce cap painted orange and purple and green.

I sat up. Don't ask me why. Perhaps to embrace the crowning.

The matching princesses saw me. They saw me together, all three of them at once. And they gave their scream together.

The chaos was more than human. I sensed I had done something wrong and tried to lie down immediately. But as I did so someone or something hit the coffin. It was set rolling and I was sent like a child in a cradle into the arms of the shouting women who scrambled to avoid me. The coffin turned and tilted, as if of its own power. It tumbled from its wheels, into the stampede of frightened women, and before I could protest my innocence I was buried in flowers; I was on the floor and under the overturned coffin. The smell of roses, the very petals themselves, closed on my nostrils. I was pleasantly surprised.

The terror in the crowd, of course, did not last long. When Sunderman and Digger got the coffin off me, I was exposed to roars of laughter. Dozens of people were bent over me, laughing. Trying to help me up.

And then someone noticed the blood on my face. My bloodied nose.

## 41

Jeremy says contemptuously that Digger and Sunderman were "a pair of stinking old bachelors" who did their batching in a shack out on the latter's homestead. They themselves had no place to sleep on that storm-bound night. And yet they were generous enough to rush the clumsy galoot to Our Lady of Sorrows Hospital; they borrowed Mr. John Backstrom's own snowmobile — on the tape Jeremy seems to call it a Sleipnir, though I can find no advertisements for such a make. They found it parked beside the Indian who was aiming an arrow at the buffalo of ice.

It started on the third kick; Digger revved it up; Jeremy was instructed to place himself on the long seat between the two men. He put his arms around Digger's belly and Sunderman put his arms around Jeremy's belly. Then they zoomed off down the street, down the trackless and almost invisible road. The wind was heaping snow in between the ridges made by the snowplows. Jeremy's nose continued to bleed as the blast of air whipped snow at their faces. He tried to hide behind Digger's parka hood, but it was no use; the blood froze in a circle around his mouth.

He must have looked more than his usual messy self when they walked into the hospital. A nurse, with the help of an attendant, got him laid out flat on a stretcher. The attendant or orderly or whatever then rolled him into a cozy little room and left him alone with the nurse.

Injured though he was, the overgrown fool had to try out his newly assumed virility. Perhaps he believed his journey northwest had not been in vain. At any rate, he resorted to the cliché that makes of every white-clad and prophylactic nurse a raving sex maniac. Had she been what Jeremy assumed, it would have been to her own unmitigated disappointment. He sniffed the intoxicating mixture of medicine and perfume that filled the air — a mixture that I have noticed does in some way stimulate unlikely appetites. She in turn rested her exquisite large breasts on his heaving chest while breathing hotly over his mouth, while washing, gently, the blood from his tender nose.

He was able to respond only by giving out one of his accustomed groans.

Laid out flat he was, so to speak, laid out flat.

Paradigm both of desire and of the desirable that he imagined himself to be, he could not accept the failed acuity of his pinpoint intention. It was then and there, stretched out under that unsuspecting and well-intentioned nurse, that he conceived — contracted — the notion that he must consult with none other than Roger Dorck. As if that huge and fallen man's very silence must communicate what words had never been able to tell our Jeremy. That man who made the finest leap might console our tumbled hero, might signal in his own disaster its own cure.

And as it happened, he had more instruction to give than ever Jeremy might have guessed.

The doctor, finally, came strolling in, announced by the shuffle of his feet. A Doctor Lipinski. He looked at the nose, poked at it, jabbed at it, pulled it, shook it, stretched it, tweaked it, jerked at it.

"Bad blow on the head," he said. "We'll have to observe him overnight."

Digger was beside himself with joy. He had finally found a place where his guest might sleep. He was also very drunk. When they were left alone in the room where Jeremy was to undress, Jeremy said wickedly to his host: "I've got to go look in on Dorck. Courtesy demands it. Just for a few minutes. I'll be right back."

"They won't allow it," Digger said.

"You have to do me a favor," Jeremy said. "Here —"

"This is insane," Digger said.

Jeremy, who had so longed for a metamorphosis of some sort,

unwittingly lent his precious self to that old gravedigger. The poor man put on the hospital gown intended for Jeremy, let Sunderman tie the knot at the back of his neck, and crawled into bed.

A new nurse came into the room. She was carrying a container of sterilized thermometers. She pulled the curtain around the bed and asked that she might be excused. Sunderman and Jeremy both said, "Of course."

"I'm going to take your temperature," the nurse said.

"Why mine?" Digger said.

"Never mind —"

"He's a little bit confused," Jeremy said. "Bad blow on the head."

"Just you relax, Mr. Sadness," the nurse said. "And turn over on your side."

Digger groaned.

"On your side," the nurse repeated. "The other way, please."

There was a pause.

"Ouch," Digger said. "What're you sticking up my ass?"

"Please, Mr. Sadness, don't move," the nurse insisted. "There. Now just you hold tight for a bit. And give me your wrist, please."

The metamorphosis, one is tempted to say, was complete. Jeremy, no longer himself, tiptoed through the door, leaving Mr. Sunderman to guard the tomb. He tiptoed down the hall and around a corner. He was tiptoeing down another hall when he met an old nun carrying a tall candle.

"Are you all right?" the nun said.

"I'm all right," Jeremy fibbed. "I don't want to wake anyone."

"Don't worry," the nun said. "They're all asleep."

"All right," he said.

"Shhh," the nun said.

"The cowboy," he said. "Where is he?"

147

"The cowboy?" the nun said. She held the candle close to his face. She might have been looking into a mirror.

"The cowboy," he said. "The cowboy."

The nun smiled brightly. "I've never seen a cowboy. Is there a cowboy here?"

"Shhh," he said.

She nodded and left. She was gone. And then he slipped into Roger Dorck's room.

## 42

There he lay, smiling to himself. Smiling, goddamnit. No, not quite; he was *almost* smiling. Enough tubes and hoses surrounding him, he looked like a moonshine still. But it was the possibility of a smile that got to me. Like you, Professor, doling out C's at the end of a semester . . .

At first I just whispered. "Dorck," I whispered, "this is enough and a little bit more. You've taken this thing too far. Other people have rights too, you know; other people take chances, get hurt, suffer."

He did nothing. He said nothing.

"Are you going to die or aren't you going to die?" I pleaded. "Dorck, we've got to know some of these things."

There he lay, motionless. I couldn't even be sure he was breathing. I didn't want to look in the direction of his chest. I studied his huge bare feet, the soles of his feet gone soft and ivory smooth, the toenails yellow as claws. The red hairs redder than ever.

And then it struck me: he was like a great Jesus bird sitting on a nest. On a cutbank ledge, on a high tree. "You're perched up there on that elevated bed, both eyes tight shut, and all the time we know you're watching." I waited. I waited for him to blink, as a bird of prey must. Only the eye betraying the held swoop, the anticipated seizure. I was a goddamned helpless mouse, trying to outwait the waiting bird. The sudden lift into nowhere. The earth itself, snatched away from my own clinging toes. "No, Dorck, I don't blame you. You've hit on a good thing, keep it going. Hatch your own conniving little schemes. . . . Outfake them all, Dorck, you fucking old king of the winter. I'm on your side. Somebody to pump in the food and somebody to syphon off the corroding waters. Fair enough. Let the damned fool humans make their damned fool human effort."

I waited again. I thought he might lunge, might swoop. I thought I had baited him into his own fatal error. The flexed muscle. The grasping claw.

"But one thing, Dorck. One damned thing. I'll go along with your fooling those other dupes and gulls. But don't try to pretend you're fooling me. Just don't lie there now pretending you've got me fooled. Because you haven't. Do you hear me? Do you hear me, Dorck? YOU HAVEN'T GOT ME FOOLED . . .

"Just once, Dorck. Just one little wink. Just one little sign of recognition, and I'll leave you alone. Don't lie there stretched out and grinning as if you've got *me* fooled. Because I see through you: you and your kind: you lazy loafing bums, you lechers and frauds and lusting old men.

"Are you *listening*, Dorck? I want you to do me a favor. I want you to die. Just goddamned die and get it over with. I can't stand this. We go around day and night waiting for one little message. He's alive. He's dead. It doesn't matter where we go, what we do. Always the question. When will the message arrive?

"Well, it's my turn to be messenger, sleepy-head. And I just brought you the big news. You're dead. From the asshole both ways, you wing-broken bird of the sun-cracked and hallooing air, you death-casting diver, you yellowing skull —

"Dorck, this is outrageous. Damn your soul. Forgive me. Bless me, father, for I have sinned. Yeah, and it's no use. Don't tell me. You don't have to tell me. Just listen. I want to say here and now that I'm sorry for everything. I was wrong. Whatever it was I did or didn't do, I confess I was dead wrong. I should have done it the other way. Whatever that is. I won't say I'll try and do better. That would be another lie. But I just want somebody to know. I'm out of step. I got off on the wrong foot. But somehow I can't bring myself to make the one little hop that would put me back in step with the goddamned marchers. I can't do it. I just want to say to somebody, *I cannot do it.*"

I opened my eyes. I found I was on my knees at the bedside of Roger Dorck.

No. I wasn't at the side of the bed. I was practically under it.

And then I noticed a suitcase. Lying there, where it wasn't supposed to be at all, I'm sure. I swear to God it was my suitcase. Like a goddamned *egg* under that calm and sitting bird. My survival kit in this humdrum world. A packed bag. It must be mine. The long journey waiting. Or maybe it was his. I was tempted to snap it open and find out. Did it contain your precious commentaries on my unwritten dissertation, Proffo? Or did it contain —

I looked up.

And then I nearly shit myself.

Roger Dorck was sitting up in bed. He was sitting up in that hollowed bed and staring — Like some aroused and hungry bird. He was watching the silent air itself. Hungry and aroused —

## 43

Poor dear Jeremy, he had his insight after all: and didn't for a moment grasp its significance. His frantic need to betray himself into death's cold clutches kept him from seeing the way to life.

His initial insight might have lit him into safety. Roger Dorck, at that moment of arousal, was more hawk than man. A fitting metaphor.

Beast of the air. Buteo. The great hatchet nose was not a nose at all but a bird's beak, hooking and sharp. No wonder he thought he might fly. The long, curled claws were feathered red to the half-moon base of their bedded nails.

I have watched those birds on a prairie day. A Swainson's hawk, poised on a telegraph pole. A red-tailed hawk, wings steady, riding the casual air. A rough-legged hawk, hovering over a gopher hole. Ferruginous and wild, the wild and waiting birds, hanging exquisite circles on an empty sky. Down they will plummet, down. The broad wings closed to a terrible descent. The knifing claws outstretched, the great beak hammering down. The wings exploding.

Jeremy, in his confused and androgynous portrait of the bird-man beast, missed the one and essential truth that any simple prairie boy might have given him. The female hawk, too, must live rapaciously. The female of that high and flaunting species may soar and swing, yes. But she too must burst and sting from that hot sky. Must plummet. Must swoop to earth, must stun and snatch the limping hare.

*Roger Dorck sat up in bed.* He stared at the staring ignoramus who had come to truth and would not dare the confabulation.

Dorck opened his mouth to what was more a faint scream than a speech.

Jeremy — again I quote him — nearly shit himself. A linguistic feat which one wishes might have been translated into mere reality. Thus he would have given himself birth into a more appropriate demise.

"Where are we?" Roger Dorck whistled out of his inhuman throat.

Jeremy Sadness hauled ass out of that room as if he had met his own soul on the high road to hell.


## 44

I had to tell Bea Sunderman. I have to. I must, I must. Warn her that he is alive.

And for that reason alone I struggled against the snow. With each floundering gesture I seemed to bury myself deeper. Only by virtue of a superhuman* effort did I stumble along on my moccasined feet. I found the big blue Sleipnir, brushed the snow off the long flat seat. I kicked the engine alive. In starting out I almost left myself behind.

And then I was in the trackless snow, making my own path. The driven snow of the blizzard cut my eyes to tearful, freezing slits in my face. I saw only the narrow space between a blank earth and a tumbling sky. I was stripped down to the animal endurance that enabled a buffalo to survive: a buffalo on the prairie, his hoofs breaking the crust of snow, his high hump holding back the storm . . .

The road beyond the northern edge of town is without lights. In the white darkness of the blizzard I was reduced to some homing instinct that resided as much in my hands as in my head. Like a cowboy, lost, I would let my horse take me home; I gave myself over to my hands on the steering gear.

Like a trapper. . . . And then I was afraid. Frightened of the inevitable circle. . . . Remembering a passage from Grey Owl: a wall of snow . . . a hissing mass of snow-devils . . . caught in the grip of one endless circle . . . the deadly circle . . . always the lost

*Only Jeremy would recognize in his every gesture the unnatural. It is in this moody and implicit commentary upon himself that he seems to recognize his failure. If not its consequence. Professor Madham.

man circling blindly, come back upon himself . . . finding himself only, his own tracks mocking him . . . the dark labyrinth become a place of phantasma and fevered imaginings . . . possessed by a shuddering dread . . . the endless circle his end —

And then I was in a forest. I was off the windswept plain and into a spruce forest. The snow no longer came at me parallel to the trackless road; now it fell like a dream onto a cushion of snow. I feared this soft invitation more than I had feared the howling wind, the knife-edged crystals that cut off my breath.

I had come to a dark house in a dark wood. I was at World's End; I turned off the engine of the snowmobile. My knees at first would not unbend; I helped them each in turn with my curled fingers.

At the door of the house I did not knock. I fell into the smothering heat.

I was alone. No one had heard me enter. I uncurled my fingers and brushed the snow from my eyelashes, rubbed the frost off my mouth, took into my lungs the scorching heat. I shook myself out of the clinging, melting snow.

Through the dark jungle of plants I felt my way, touching now a mistletoe cactus, now a potted palm. Carefully I extricated myself from the embrace of a climber that was swinging its tentacles in the dark air. A cat leaped from something, somewhere, onto my shoulder. I damned near strangled on my own impulse to cry out. I reached for my microphone, desperate to whisper into its ass's ear: I checked the impulse. The silence held.

Without a light, only touching the rail under its covering of ivy, then reaching to touch the bare steps themselves, I climbed the long stair. Climbed upward and on, as if I must soon surface out of the black silence.

I found the hallway. The silence trailed behind me like a cat, eager to pounce. . . . No. The silence in no way trailed me. It was already there, ahead of me. My fingers touched the cold outline of a doorway. I found the door. Then, attempting to enter the room that I was sure was empty, I bumped a clock. I was looking for an empty room. A clock was ticking. I fumbled to stop it. In trying to stop it I bumped another: that clock too, in the darkness, began to tick. Drip. Stutter. Tap. Thump. Like a drum. . . . No no no. It was ticking. Only ticking. But more than ticking. Deliberately I set a third clock to going. Running. Ha. As if the sound of the third must hide that of the first and second. The tight, inhuman voices of the clocks were a screen against all sound.

Then I heard footsteps. Footsteps like the ticking of a clock. I thought I heard footsteps. Except I was not sure if they were growing louder or softer. They were as regular as the ticking of a clock.

Don't ask me why: I climbed into the bed. I felt my way into the invisible bed. I lay down flat on my back, fully clothed, under the sheet and quilt. I wondered if my moccasins were clean and dry. I folded my hands on my chest.

If I had heard steps, then I no longer heard them. Of this I am certain, however: a clock that had not been ticking began to tick. I might have frozen to death that instant, under a quilt in a warm room, fully dressed. Somewhere, now, I could hear my own heart. Or was it a clock I heard?

And then a hand found me. Touched, in the darkness, my groin. Three fingers touched me. I felt each finger distinctly. Then they withdrew.

All thinking had swooned from my mind. I was as blank as the darkness around me, I could not see. Perhaps I had closed my eyes. I could only hear. I might have been drowning in that darkness. I could not open my mouth.

She was undressing. Under all the ticking of the clocks I heard a woman's heel tap once and securely on the hard floor.

She was calmly undressing at my bedside: that woman whose footsteps I had heard, whose hand had found me.

I thought of myself lying there, fully clothed. Enough clothes between my flesh and the world to see me through a raging blizzard. Only I was snug in bed. Jeremy Bentham came to my mind. Dressed fit to kill and embalmed and wearing his own wax head in his goddamned little showcase at the foot of the stairs in his famous little university. Jeremy Bentham, I said to myself, you plodding visionary, I see it all now: the greatest pleasure of the most ordinary man is the greatest happiness of the greatest number. And the greatest happiness of the greatest number of ordinary men is to lie down.

Yes. I was thinking again. After all. And the greatest lying down is the lying down of the ordinary man. . . . I was paralyzed into thought. I was once again a total stranger to my own prick. I was at a dead loss as to what I must do.

She had undressed; she was standing naked and invisible beside the bed. That invisible woman. Standing still at the bed's head.

She gave to the whole room the smell of earth; not of flowers only but the dark breathing silence of ferns in crevices of rock. The lichens, orange and yellow, on a rotting limb. The green moss, cool to the sliding mouse. The smell of a northern forest, where the snow melts itself black into the last shade. The muskeg waters of the north, cold and bottomless and darker brown than any handful of clay, redolent of all our beginnings. The deserted nest. The beaver dam, broken. The only trail, and that one hardly more than the track of a stalked hare, the stalking lynx. The forgotten signal on the still air. The mating coyotes. The smoke of a burning prairie. The bones of a buffalo not long dead, and the grass and the crocus and the first violet, stemming sweet from that final odor. The blinding sun on our nostrils. The high of our own last hunger.

I could not make a move.

I was moving.

She was standing, still, and I was moving.

The Columbus quest for the oldest New World. The darkest gold. The last first. I was lifting my hidden face. To the gateway beyond. To the place of difficult entrance. To the real gate to the dreamed cave. The dream cave's lost mouth, encompassing the compass. To the castle buried in thorns; the unkissed princess awaiting the kiss. The loot and swag of all marauding. The hunted forest on the cant hill. The rabbitty warren. The sapsucker raiding the broken tree. The pussyfoot lair of the mountain lion. The treasure troll. The diver downed. The snatching shark. The lava lapping, into the sea. At the volcano's lip, the sweet stench, the scorched charisma of the mountainous hole.

I had tongued the unspeakable silence.

"I have waited," she said. To the darkness. Under the ticking of the clocks. "You came back. I have been waiting. It was a long time."

I could not tell her. I could not tell her anything. I believed then, I believe, she took me for her lost husband. Her lost young husband, vanished, supposed to be dead. Come back from the freezing water. All those years she had been waiting and now he had returned to the bed that was kept for him. She had waited and she had waited. As if every woman in the world kept a bed, not for a husband, not for her everyday lover, but for the mysterious youth who one night years ago walked into the darkness, vanished from the very surface of the earth. The finest prospect. The perfect physique. And after all the waiting of all those women, one figure had returned. Finally. At last.

And then I made a discovery.

Old Man. Diogenes. Ill Omen. Shipwreck. Dancer or Drum. Call him what you will. He was up.

I was in bed. I had an erection.

156

I was lying down, stretched out flat, and that strange voyager who accompanies all my catastrophes was up like a mast: like a mast and a sail.

To speak would be to boast. And I was speechless. Perhaps I roared. I am not certain now. I did not moan. To say that we were joined, Bea and I, would be, once again, to underline the failure of language. We were welded in the smithy of our mutual desire. Fused in the bellowed flame. Tonged and hammered. . . . No no no no no no. I have ransacked my twenty-five years of education for a suitable metaphor. I have done a quick review of logic, called upon the paradigms of literature and history. I have put to test the whole theory of a liberal education.

Nothing.

Absolutely nothing.

I only know that for a long, long time I had not heard the ticking clocks.

"How was it for you?" Bea said.

Only then did I speak. Only then did I betray my voice. Reluctantly, I spoke. "I am pleased," I said. "And for you?"

She replied with a kiss to my listening ear. "I am pleased," she said.

And she did not move away from me. We lay together, flabbergasted together.

And that was when I recognized: I will never ever get out of bed, get up again. Never. Not ever. I am bedbound. Freed finally from the curse of locomotion. Ha. The free man freed from his freedom. The curse cursed. Yes. Now. I shall, at last, commence my dissertation. Christopher Columbus, not knowing that he had not come to the Indies of his imagination. Imagined that he had come to the Indies.

Right on, Sadness. Dead center. The beautiful truth. The inevitable opening for which the tuned ear inevitably listens.

Dissertation Number Eleven: "The Plot Against Plot".

I am landing all over again. The wheels rumble into position. Extinguish your cigarette. *Boucler les ceintures SVP*. Put the back of your seat in an upright position. The mechanical voice has got to be kidding: Edmonton International Airport it says, in English, then in French. Down below our jet engines we see nothing but snow-drifted fields. The setting sun a blood clot in my own glass skull. The small earth downward and darkly white —

Blank.

I lie here. Ha. I am going to lie here for the rest of my life, talking, recording everything. Until I can think nothing that I do not speak. Speaking. Until the inside and the outside are one, united — The clocks are striking. One of them says it is six o'clock. One of them says it is either midnight or noon.

Dissertation Number Twelve: "The Quest Unquestioned".

"Jeremy?"

"Yes."

"Will you answer the telephone?"

"Good God, no. Not now."

"Please. Answer that awful phone."

"Never. I am never going to get out of bed. Not ever. Not until — Listen to me. Come back. . . . I am bedbound. Freed finally . . . into bed . . . forever . . . until a new ice age . . . the slow southward push . . . I refuse . . . the glacier itself, nudging the bedpost . . . slowly . . . I refuse . . . forcing the bed itself, sideways, up . . . CAN YOU HEAR ME? . . . the old glacier itself, the primal stuff in primal motion . . . come back . . . slowly breaking my happy trance . . . the tumble and rattle of terminal moraine, the distant thunder of ice; cracking . . . the immeasurable assault . . . COME BACK . . . the tongue of ice slipping over the horizon's lip . . . slanting away from the Pole itself . . . the blue-green flame advancing . . . the river of ice . . . the rammed, blunt needle —"

# 45

Jeremy swore he would never get out of bed. One thinks immediately of Goncharov's Oblomov. That same night the stolen snowmobile was found on the cowcatcher of a locomotive, smashed almost beyond identification; both Jeremy and Bea had disappeared. Thus, Miss Sunderman, what you in your letter refer to as "the mystery".

That the bodies were not to be found is no mystery to me, I assure you. Could I but persuade Jeremy's wife of the truth of my realization, I would be free to dismiss the trifle from my mind; as it is I must, impatiently, take a harder look at the matter. I am certain that Jeremy and Bea were killed. Carol, unfortunately, persists in the notion that her husband faked the two deaths.

It would seem apparent that the tape recorder itself, and not what was recorded on its tape, tells the whole story. The recorder was found dangling from a timber in the middle of the famous old Ketchamoot Bridge. That trestle bridge — and I have checked the original records of the now defunct Grand Trunk Pacific to get the exact details — is apparently one of the largest of its kind in the world. To be more exact, it measures 3,992 feet in length, from rim to rim of the Cree River valley; in vertical dimension the four tiers of crossed and braced log-work, along with the pony deck, measure 145 feet from the single set of rails down to the river flats. It is recorded that four million feet of timber and 162 tons of bolts were used in the erection of the trestle; 150 men labored from dawn to dusk, through a winter and a summer. During the actual nine months of construction, only two men fell to their deaths.

Which brings me to Carol's little bone of contention.

In the case of Bea and Jeremy, no crushed and broken bodies were in evidence at the base of that veritable cliff of neatly patterned poles and braces.

Indeed not.

The tape recorder was discovered hanging by its strap from a bolt on a timber 144 feet *directly* above the surface of the Cree River. An accident of the accident.

I hesitate to call to your mind the thought of your own mother and her lover falling; but fall they surely did. Perhaps indeed they saw the train before the moment of impact: together they leapt, clinging together as they had clung in their fornications; together they fell, turning in the dark and storm-torn night, writhing and twisting in vain, calling out to the deaf night, asking for a stay that could not be granted, slamming onto the sculptured and smithereened ice. Cracking through to the gush of black and freezing water beneath the appalling surface.

I see it only too well.

Carol, however, carried away by her imagination, would have the conspirators planting the snowmobile on the track, then scurrying away to catch the train when it stopped, which in truth it did.

The engineer, recognizing that his engine had struck something in the blinding storm, brought his train to a halt and sent a brakeman back onto the bridge; a delay that cost the already delayed train another precious hour. He himself examined the smashed snowmobile, looking for hairs or frozen blood. Carol would have it that during that time the couple boarded the train and found a roomette. She would have them further pursuing their greed for each other's bodies, even while the train moved again into the continuing darkness.

Carol, in her own delightful way, fails to grasp the consequence of the northern prairies to human definition: the diffusion of personality into a complex of possibilities rather than a concluded self. She is a Binghamton girl, grew up protected by hills and by trees — even if her wise mother, as the saying has it, *threw her out.* When she fell for her finch and popinjay version of Jeremy.

We were stretched out in Jeremy's bed on the third day of Hurricane Agnes, which had become by then a mere tropical storm.

"Why are you so depressed?" Carol said.

"I'm not depressed. I'm happy."

"You're depressed."

"It's this fucking Binghamton weather. This endless overcast. I feel that I'm suffocating — we're all suffocating in this place, saturated, walled in, drowning."

"Get up," she said. "Get out of bed."

"I can't," I said. "And I'm not depressed, I'm happy. What do you expect me to do, run out naked from this happy place?"

She refuses the possibility of marriage, on the grounds that it might constitute an *act* of bigamy. A foolish quibble. But fortunately, after that exchange, I was able to persuade her to give up the apartment and move into a room in my house. She has, thanks to me also, been able to give up her menial task in the Xerox Room of the University. She shares my passion for antiques and now she is able to spend a good many hours cleaning and restoring our precious objects, shopping around in the hills for more: she will on occasion disappear for the whole day. . . . And yet one must grant the dear girl her question: What *were* Bea and Jeremy doing on the bridge?

That, too, is clear enough to me.

Jeremy couldn't steer a toy wagon in broad daylight. What happened in the blizzard? He got lost.

Carol, of course, has fabricated a wonderful tale for herself: knowing Jeremy's passion to become an aboriginal of some variety, she supposes he was quite recklessly and irrationally heading for the true wilderness. I have explained to her that, yes, she is right in insisting that the railway company in question maintains a scheduled run across the continent. And trains on that run would in fact pass through wilderness, of sorts. But *that particular train*, because of snow-bound tracks — and the records themselves are apparently confused — was both *off schedule* and using a track it was not supposed to be *on*.

She, nevertheless, would have her romantic couple stepping down from their long and snow-scarred Pullman the very next day, the day after: getting off the train at a whistle stop on the prairies. Or in the forest to the east of the prairies. Or in the mountains to the west. She would have them hop down from the train, even as Grey Owl and Anahareo might have jumped headlong out of a boxcar with their few surviving beaver. With all the unbounded wilderness rolling to the north. Making a clean break into the last forest. Into a valley. Harnessing a dog team and breaking a new trail. Building a raft, floating down north on the spring break-up. Seeking the last unbroken muskrat lodge, the unfished lake of trout and jack, the circle of buffalo, bending to drink. . . . No," I told her. "Not ever."

We were getting into my car, driving up to the Ross Park Zoo to picnic on the grass. "I rode that train," I explained to her. "I came east on that same line, rode through a hard winter. I waved at the section hands who only stood stock still in the blistering cold air and let me go. I saw the rivers running north. Under the ice and snow: locked —"

"I would have gone with him," Carol interrupted.

It is that kind of silliness that intrudes upon reason. Carol argues that Jeremy saw the bridge while participating in the snowshoe race and recognized the means of fraud for which he had been searching. . . . I *know* that he was only running away, and *accidentally* hit upon the bridge. Jeremy had difficulty with a pencil sharpener. If you told him where north is, he couldn't for the world find south.

He quite simply got lost, trying to find Notikeewin. It was a brutal night out; I know that kind of prairie blizzard. The snow sweeps for unbroken miles, parallel to the bleak white earth. Jeremy was lost in the space of his own choosing; he hit on the railway track. He followed it, which was sensible in its own way. If you understand that in such vastness even a railway only *seems* to have direction.

One can surely conceive of the two of them, Jeremy and Bea, Bea clinging to her Indian lover, he bent behind the pathetic windscreen, staying between the two black ribbons of steel, following to nowhere. . . . That Jeremy disappeared is a pity. Why Bea Sunderman went with him might ask a little more accounting for. It grieves me to think that Worlds End (and I abjure the apostrophe) is now deserted. I feel that I have, in listening to your hero, in ordering his fragments of tape (and I had to destroy them, finally; they were cluttering up my office), come to love that old house as well as if it were my own.

Where was I, yes —

To get on to the question of why a young man should, in the first place, wish to run off and leave behind him a young wife. Carol speculates that his — as she puts it, *disappearance* — is the ultimate expression of his repeated concern for "the great god Tit". That particular god to whom he attributed the bestowing of all grants, fellowships, assistantships, six-hour teaching loads and lecherous female office mates — that god is obviously, as Carol remarks, a goddess. And that goddess is the lost mother. And the lost mother represents — forgive me, but I must say it out — the cunt he was always trying so unsuccessfully to get back into. I personally feel he was a self-deluded little asshole (in spite of his height) who should have been strangled at birth. Or set on a hillside to perish. I only wish he had drowned in his mother's bathtub. Or got himself killed by a drug-hungry black in the streets of that city from which he fled ever westward. I sent him out there. . . .

But I was venturing a guess as to what happened. Is that not the final question, speculate as one may? What, I ask, happened? Not, what is it? Not, who is it? Not. . . . When Bea answered the phone. . . .

We have only the tape recorder, and in it the last tape, the cassette you sent in response to my request. Jeremy is raving on about how he is going to stay in bed forever. Bea goes to answer the telephone. Jeremy cannot hear her on the phone, mostly because of his preoccupation with the sound of his own voice. Bea comes back to the bed and says, *"He's alive —"*

## 46

Miss Sunderman, Roger Dorck's loss of memory is for me a terrible accident. Only he could truly clear up the matter of the phone call. I must trust the veracity of your, let me say, generally *delightful* letter (and please feel free to write again soon). But you say he cannot remember making the call, or asking that it be made, because he cannot remember a single detail of his life dating from *the moment before he learned of his friend's — of Robert Sunderman's — death.*

It would surely seem impossible that anyone might drown in all that ice and snow. God knows, I shall never forget it. And yet, Robert Sunderman went through the ice. Or knocked a hole in the ice and disappeared. . . . No; it is just possible. A night in late fall, a thin coat of snow, the ice deserted, darkness . . . his child-bride pregnant, the boy-husband alone, already regretting the boyhood that he could not quite surrender . . . the perfect physique, the absolute potential . . . thinking and not thinking, chasing the puck across the new ice. . . .

Incidentally, that Mr. Dorck mistakes you for your mother, a woman he remembers as being young and beautiful beyond the powers of the human imagination; that his amnesia restores a lost perfection has, somehow, overtones of the tragic. And that he now worships you even as he worshipped her before her impulsive marriage to the "perfect physique" of Robert Sunderman is also to be lamented. Yet I see even in these most pitiful events, in this saddest forgetting, the benevolence of a generous Creator. . . . Now poor Roger is out of the hospital and able to share your city apartment. I imagine for both of you a kind of tranquility in that lasting return to a golden youth. . . .

"He is alive," Bea said. Jeremy fell silent. He turned off his tape recorder. He punched it dead.

I am persuaded that the shameless pair were newly become prisoners of their new-scratched flesh: they would kiss and paw and suck at each other's bodies forever. They seized together some clothes for their naked backs, filled their pockets with money. They squatted onto the stolen snowmobile; Jeremy fumbled the machine alive.

And they rode away seeking NOTHING. They sought NOTHING. They would FLEE everything. THEY DID NOT KNOW WHERE THEY WERE GOING.

Together and alone, blinded by desire, they had no thought of consequence or pain. They did not consider family, friends, community, the benediction of the living, the graves of their dead. They did not think to the next minute, let alone to the next day. They saw only a gap in the fence, a gate left open, a padlock sprung. And out they went. Into the blizzard.

Lost.

Lost and together, they followed the night. They were lost and knew they were lost and did not know they were lost. They followed their own little light. One can conceive of their hitting, quite by chance, the pair of steel tracks in the lifting snow.

They are lost and yet they have beneath them the assurance of steel rails that must and do go somewhere. They follow, and they follow. They come to the bridge. Jeremy feels security because he has seen the bridge before. Ah, that feeling of at-homeness, born of familiar appearance. The Ketchamoot Bridge, he tells himself. He knows the name. He knows that great wall of timber and iron.

They head out onto the level bridge. The earth falls away beneath them. The spruce trees, darker than the storm, fall into a coulee. The buried saskatoon bushes are gone. The rim of the valley fades on the night.

They ride out onto the narrow bridge as if they are levered into the very sky itself: in the huge night there is no earth beneath them, only the lash of snow in their little light; they are freed of the earth, airborne, flying free.

They are approaching the middle of the bridge. Led by their own little headlight. They see in the darkness before them a light as small as their own. A small faint inviting light that swells on the darkness, burns in the lash of snow.

She is holding him in her arms. Bea, on the snowmobile seat, holds him in her arms. Perhaps he is even warm. Warm and secure. I have thought of that too. Perhaps what really matters is the warmth each finds in the other's body. Two bodies. Warm. The rest is fiction. . . .

But even the whine of the snowmobile cannot deny the roaring shadow that comes to the bridge and will cross it. And they cannot hide and they cannot turn, Jeremy and Bea. They cannot turn back. The train comes on, indifferent. Into the indifferent storm. And they have time to see it, Jeremy and Bea. They have time to see the unbearable indifference. Unbearable and sweet. They have that much time. As the beaver might, its foot in the

166

trap. The antelope, turning to lick the bloodied arrow. The buffalo, driven to the cliff's blue edge.

The water below is indifferent; through a labyrinth of rivers and lakes, it falls off and down, to Hudson Bay, to Baffin Island, to the drifting Arctic wastes.

They leap.

They leap from the iron path. From the spanning bridge. From the closing lights. Together they fall, clinging to nothing but each other's regret, spilling down the sudden sluice, the dark incurious flume, their eyes alive to the nail-point snow, their tongues unhinged in the whistling night.

They are lovers.

They do not even scream as they fall.